STICK NO BILLS

ELIZABETH WALCOTT-HACKSHAW

STICK NO BILLS

SHORT STORIES

PEEPAL TREE

First published in Great Britain in 2020
Peepal Tree Press Ltd
17 King's Avenue
Leeds LS6 1QS
England

ISBN13: 9781845234676

Supported using public funding by
ARTS COUNCIL
ENGLAND

CONTENTS

For David, Dylan and Amy

I: ASHES

GROS ISLET

She was walking forward, going back, back in her mind to see the old man, the one they called Captain, sitting on the bench, the same bench that he sat on every afternoon at five o'clock. She could see him cross the road at the traffic lights, walk his bike across the three lanes and then up onto the pavement, toward his two friends already seated on their Savannah bench – Bird Man with the birdcage right in front of him, and the one they called Express, hiding behind his newspapers. These two always left a space on the far right for Captain and his bike. On many afternoons they'd passed him in his cap, crisp white short-sleeved shirt, loose-fitting navy-blue trousers, heavy black-framed glasses, his pale skin liver-spotted, though the hair showing from beneath his cap was jet black. There was always an old portable antenna radio slung across the handle-bars of his bike. Captain must have been at least seventy-five. Bird Man, with his aquiline nose and charcoal skin, sat upright to keep an eye on his bird directly in front of him; Express always hid behind his newspaper, but she could see his thin arms and hands – a muddy brown, tracked with thick veins. Express wore brogues, Captain, white trainers, and Bird Man, a pair of flip-flops.

She had woken up at five that morning in the darkness. Her room was on the ground floor of the hotel; it opened onto the pool. She slid open the door, felt the cool morning air on her face, heard the birds and a swishing sound – probably a groundsman, but she couldn't see anyone. She went to lie down again, to go back to sleep, but her thoughts were already running away from her. Her cell phone was on the night stand, and she wanted to call him, ask if he missed her, if he had taken his afternoon walk around the Savannah, if he had seen Captain, Bird Man and Express. Instead she began to prepare for the day by turning on the lights, taking her dress off the hanger and spreading it across the bed. She had bought it only two days before, an impulse buy as she rushed around the malls, changing dollars from TT to EC. The dress had looked so lovely on the mannequin in the shop window. An aquamarine sheath in a light silk, loose-fitting and perfect for the occasion; it made her think of the sea or the sky. She was dressed and ready by 6:15 but breakfast was not until 7:00, so she decided to walk around the hotel grounds. In a few hours the hotel would come to life with guests, workers, lawn mowers, weed whackers, but now it felt still, even empty. She heard movement around her as more souls emerged with the light. He would be getting ready for work, waiting for the first caregiver to arrive so that he could leave his mother, who barely recognised him now, her firstborn son. She hadn't asked him to come with her. He'd offered, but she knew he couldn't leave. He was finally beginning to realise that he would soon have to put his mother into a home; even with his sister's help, his aunt's, his uncle's and the many caregivers, it was too much. His mother had managed to unlatch the gate, wander off and had been found sitting in a neighbour's porch. When she was eating she could no longer be trusted to hold a glass, wipe her mouth or remember to chew. They were always changing caregivers because she would accuse them of stealing any and everything. Every part of his life, their life together, was being taken away.

She was glad he hadn't come with her. This was something she had to do alone and, besides, this island was supposed to be her home away from home; she had family here above and below ground, as her uncle would say: she had buried a grandmother, an aunt, an uncle and two cousins. She had said many Hail Marys in her favourite cemetery – the one that faced the sea. Her mother's ashes were there as well; her mother had always said she wanted to be next to her mother and sister. Her mother had relatives all over the island from Cap to Castries to Choiseul. But this island was her mother's home, not hers; she did not feel she belonged, even if she wished she did.

She walked towards the main desk in the hotel lobby. "*Bonjour*," she said as she passed every hotel worker. From a child she had been taught to say "*bonjour*" before anything else. "*Bonjour, Madame*" to the waitress who poured her coffee and "*Bonjour, Madame*" to the lady who took her dirty breakfast plate. The lady at the desk took her keys and smiled widely. "*Bonjour, Madame, bonne journée.*" The lady must have thought she was Martinican and that she had relatives here – as many Martinicans did. Martinique was just fifteen minutes by plane, an hour or so by ferry. Her mother would say that the family was Caribbean – not St Lucian, not Grenadian, not Dominican, not Trinidadian, just Caribbean. Her mother never mentioned the Bajan side, never mentioned the island where her mother had met her father and where her mother left him. She had only seen her father a few times, and had never met her father's other family. The Bajan half-brother and half-sisters remained ghosts.

She left the hotel, saying a very polite "No thank you" to the taxi drivers outside; she would walk. The hotel was located just off the main road. She stayed at the side of the road until the pavement suddenly stopped, then she walked on the gravel. They didn't know that she would be coming early; she wanted to surprise them. They had begged her to stay with them at the house but she'd refused; the house was already full of other family members who had flown in to celebrate her uncle's seventy-fifth birthday. She didn't want to call to say she was on her way because they would fuss, say it was too hot, want to send the driver, Mac could be there in ten minutes – no, it would be better this way, and they would have a story to tell for the rest of the day – of her walk from the hotel, through Gros Islet to the house.

She passed tourists walking along the road, on their way to the beach, their faces pink with the heat. As the maxi-taxi drivers drove past her, with passengers spilling out of the windows, they honked their horns, slowing to see if she wanted to get in. She must have looked very strange to them, dressed up this way and walking along the road. She seldom walked when she visited her family here; they would never let her. If Mac couldn't take her wherever she wanted to go, they would take her. Renting a car would have been rude; it meant that they hadn't provided her with enough transport, that in some way they had failed to take care of her needs. So with each step she felt freer and emboldened by her decision. She passed the gas station, the groceries, the marina, the fruit stalls, coconut carts and vendors; she heard two ladies waiting at the bus stop say something as she walked by, but she didn't speak Creole well enough anymore to understand. They must have thought she was a little crazy to be walking in this heat, especially in that nice dress.

She started up the hill and she saw the sign for horse rides down to *Case en Bas* where people went to wade and soak the horses' hot bodies in the water. When she and her younger brother spent their August holidays here with their cousins, they would always have a day dedicated to a horse ride down to *Case en Bas*. One set of aunts, uncles, mothers and fathers would drive down to the beach to wait for the other set to arrive on horseback; the older children would be given a horse each, the younger ones would have a parent in the saddle with them. To finally be in the saddle alone was a great mark of distinction among the cousins; it determined the pecking order for the rest of the vacation. The older cousins could now order the younger ones to do their bidding – fetching snorkel and masks, taking leaves and frogs out of the pool, picking up beach balls and doing any chore the adults wanted them to do.

She had always felt safe in the saddle, was never afraid like some of her younger cousins; she sat upright with good form and controlled the horse well. Her mother had always said she was too brave; in her mother's world this was not always a good thing. Her mother had warned her that sometimes it was okay to be afraid; there was need in life for both courage and fear. Fear would keep her daughter safe, make her stay away from drugs, alcohol and bad men. "God shields our eyes with scales so we do not see what is around the corner. God protects us from seeing all the bad to come." She was not like her mother, had made it a point not to be. But lately her mother's words had begun to haunt her. She would have given anything to recapture that powerful feeling she once had atop that beautiful mare trotting down the hill to *Case en Bas*.

She could feel her skin burning, smell the car fumes. There was no shade on the main road. But soon she would turn into Gros Islet and the trees and houses would provide some shelter. Most of the ladies were sitting outside their homes or small shops; the men were already in the bars along the road drinking their Pitons, or rum. One vagrant, no older than twenty, a drug addict, was dancing outside a bar in front of the tall speakers blasting *soca* from Trinidad. The men outside the bar were encouraging her to raise her skirt a little higher; you could already see her breasts under the torn shirt. The vagrant's skin was caked with dirt and her hair stuck together in clumps. Two older ladies opposite the bar were pointing at her accusingly, but they never took their eyes off her snakelike moves. Suddenly her cellphone rang; it startled her, releasing her from the vagrant's spell.

"Hey. Where are you now?" he said. "I called your room in the hotel but there was no answer."

"I decided to walk."

"Walk where?"

"To the house; it's not that far. I didn't want to bother them. How's your mother?"

"Okay. She was good yesterday, no drama."

"That's good."

"I wanted to tell you that I found out his name."

"Whose name?"

"Captain's – check this, his name is Lazarus."

"Who the hell would call their son Lazarus?"

"Long story, I'll tell you when you come back. You are coming back, right?"

"Why would I come back? I have everything I need right here."

He laughed, but she wanted him to say, *Come back to me, come back for me.* "I can pick you up tomorrow night, same time, right?"

"Right." And the call ended with their usual *love yous*.

She put the phone back into her bag and took a few steps, still hearing his voice in her head. Then she saw it and stopped: the Gros Islet church. It was one of her mother's favourites. Whenever her mother was staying with her brother, she would attend mass at the Gros Islet church.

Her mother had attended mass at the church on that Sunday morning. That same Sunday night, on her return to Trinidad, as she was driving home from the airport, a truck broke a red light and their lives were never the same. Her mother had gone to St Lucia to celebrate her brother's big seventieth birthday bash. That was five years ago, and for those five years her uncle could not think of his birthday without tying it to his sister's death. But this year he had decided that it was time to remember his sister's life rather than her death, and so the family would stop their mourning and begin to celebrate two lives, his sister's and his own.

She had planned to go inside the church; that was one of the reasons she wanted to walk. She would go inside and light a candle for her mother. She didn't. Churches always made her feel uncomfortable; she was always too aware of herself, even as a little girl – kneeling, the sign of cross, the sign of peace, the holy water, the Our Father – she'd done them all to please her mother, and she simply couldn't bring herself to do it anymore, not even today. She made the sign of the cross and then kept walking towards the small bridge.

After crossing the bridge, she had a choice: to walk along the beach lined with shady trees or go back onto the main road. The road would have been faster, but the light on the turquoise water pulled her towards the beach. She took off her sandals to feel the sand mixed with small shells and pieces of coral. Under some of the trees there were wooden tables and benches. She decided to sit for a moment. The bay was filled with yachts flying flags; she could make out a French flag, a British one and an Italian; there were two others but she wasn't sure – one could have been German. A family was swimming in the shallow water – a father, mother and two sons – taking an early morning sea bath. Two guards from the hotel were sitting on white plastic chairs put out for the hotel guests, many of whom were already on the beach.

Suddenly, she thought she heard a shriek, and that was when she saw a woman in the water, laughing and telling her to come in. "Bring a mango," she said, then added, "Bring two." She'd loved to eat mangoes in the water, with the sea's salt.

"I don't have a towel," she called back.

"Doesn't matter. The sun will dry you off, come in. It's perfect, not cold at all, nice and warm."

She wanted to go into the water, swim with the woman and eat a mango (how did she know she had two mangoes in her bag, stolen from the buffet table at breakfast?), but she got up and turned away from the beach, her back to the water and the woman calling her.

She crossed the field where the horses were, avoiding the thorns in the brushes; she could see Pigeon Island in the distance; she could see the rocks, the waves, and a sailboat. As she walked across the cricket field she recognized the jeep coming toward her. It was Mac.

"Good day, Miss Suzanne, I now on my way to look for you at the hotel. Your aunt and uncle trying to call you all morning."

"Mac, *bonjour*, you good? I just wanted to take a little walk. You know how they like to worry."

"Is too hot for a walk, Miss Suzanne. Come I'll take you back to the house."

"I want to surprise them; let me walk, it's just up the hill."

Mac didn't insist; he couldn't insist she get into the jeep.

"Wait until I get up to the house and then come; otherwise they will hear the noise from the jeep."

Mac did as she requested. He waited in the field until he saw her disappear.

She walked up the driveway, passed the guest house and went higher up the hill to the main house. She could hear her aunt and uncle in the kitchen. When her aunt looked up from the sink and saw her, she ran outside. Her uncle soon followed. They looked surprised, worried, and then happy.

"You Trinis mad, *oui*," her aunt said, hugging her; it had been two years since she had seen her niece. "We're so glad you came, but why you didn't call us? We could have come for you – the hotel is so far to walk all that way." All the while her aunt kept holding her.

"Let the child go; you want to spoil her lovely dress?"

It was now her uncle's turn to hold her.

"Happy Birthday, Uncle," she said. He held on tighter and she could feel his body start to shake. He pulled away and laughed.

"You know, he's so happy to see you he's beside himself, just old age, you know," her aunt said. All three laughed as they walked into the house.

They made her eat a second breakfast, made her rest although she wasn't really tired. And during the party that day they would tell the story over and over again, about Suzanne's walk from the hotel through Gros Islet. She laughed, reminisced with her cousins about the old days; they spoke about the family, how much the clan had grown. Her younger cousins ran around the garden and got into trouble the way their mothers and fathers used to when they were their age. When the *en bas gorge* band began to play, her aunt and uncle danced on the lawn. He danced with his daughters and granddaughters too, and then her uncle came and held out his hand to her.

The music and the singing carried her thoughts back to the beach, and as they waltzed across the lawn, her uncle said to her, "You know I think she's here today."

"Yes," she replied, "and she's dancing away."

KILLING TIME

In the empty car park, protected by a fortress of hills from the Paramin valley, the parked flatbed truck is full of neat mounds of mangoes, pawpaws, portugals, pomme de cytheres, avocados, tomatoes and watermelon. Her lanky fruit man stands in front of the scales in his usual black T-shirt and faded Levis, a machete in his belt, and the usual wry smile. He doesn't turn to look at her when she says "Good morning". He's focused on weighing slightly bruised bananas for the customer he's serving, a thin old man with stark white hair that looks like a shimmering halo around his dark brown face. The old man smiles at her. He pays her fruit man, takes his bananas and wishes her fruit man and herself a good day in that old-time way. The old man walks towards the Paramin hills, disappears around the corner, fading like a shadow, a ghost.

Her fruit man turns to her; it's her turn now and for the first time she notices that the index finger is missing from his left hand. It's strange that she's never noticed that brown nodule before; perhaps she had always imagined a finger. The fruit man looks at her without saying a word; she has already selected a heap of Julie mangoes and two avocadoes. He takes them from her, slightly brushing her fingers, puts them in a bag and tells her how much she owes. The transaction is never filled with wasted words or small talk, but it is never unpleasant. Her fruit man has the look of someone who knows things about this world that she may never know. He looks as though he has all the answers, all the secret codes, powers she will never possess in this life or the next. As she puts her wallet back into her handbag she has to stop herself from staring at the missing finger.

★

Best lunch in the world, her father used to say, Julie mangoes and avocadoes. All she needs now is something to read because she'd finished her book last night, by a Jamaican novelist. A critic had described the prose as "athletic" and she liked that. Lean, athletic, sounded kind of sexy. She can't think of another book in that box in her new apartment that she wants to read, so she decides to pass by the book shop.

★

The hotel carpark is empty. She parks next to the main entrance; the clouds are heavy, grey and angry. Angry clouds – that might work in her poem, so she makes a mental note. She has been working on two poems for her three-week creative writing course. "Rain" is the working title of the first poem, but she isn't sure about the other one, still untitled.

Walking into the tiny bookshop, the smell of tobacco, a nice, sweet-pipe smell; it made her think of her father again. But "nice" is not a good word, she should try to find better words, less common words; "musty" or "woodsy" are definitely much better. The foreign lady is there, with her leathery, puffy skin, her smoker's yellow hands, hunched over some book hidden below the counter. This foreign lady is often in the book shop, but she is not the owner; the foreign lady is helpful but not as friendly as the owner. She doesn't bother to move from where she is sitting. But no help is needed; she knows these shelves well, knows all the spines, all the images on the covers, she can spot a new edition right away. Browsing the shelves dedicated to international authors she can't find one title that she hasn't seen before, but the foreign authors are always few and far between; the bookstore specializes in Caribbean books. On these shelves there is only one new poetry title, *Words from the Heart*. The syrupy title makes her move immediately to the novels, two new ones from Jamaica and then the usual suspects: Kincaid, Lovelace, Naipaul. The book idea is fading fast. "Okay, thank you," she says to Ms Foreign Lady, who mumbles something, barely looking up from her book.

★

August vacation, no traffic around the Queen's Park Savannah even at lunch time. Terrific, she thinks, a word her father liked to say. But, as if on cue, the clouds burst terrifically and the terrific rain begins to pelt down on the windshield; mixed with the heat, the roads have a layer of steam. Thank goodness the apartment bedroom is air-conditioned. When she gets home she plans to eat her mangoes on the floor in the cool room, but not before she makes a vinaigrette for the avocadoes. After the meal she'll drink some cough medicine that warns about drowsiness (she finished all of the wine the night before) and hopefully pass out for a few hours.

There are a few boys in school uniforms braving the rain as she passes her favourite coconut cart opposite the Queen's Royal College. Her cell phone starts to ring. It's somewhere in her bag, she doesn't try to find it to ID the number and it doesn't ring a second time, but she hears the blip of a text. He must be suffering. Good, let him suffer, he's a dog, a frigging cur. She is getting stronger and stronger every day, every hour. It has been three weeks since she last saw him. If only it wasn't raining she would stop for a coconut water, just to kill time. These days she has too much time to kill and her TV died in the move to her new apartment.

Her brother left for New York last Sunday; she feels as though he took away a good chunk of her courage in that new fancy four-wheel suitcase of his. He made her promise at the airport not to go back. "Never liked that jackass." Her brother always referred to him as "that jackass ... Never trusted him. We see things that you all don't; we can spot an ass miles away." She knows he's right, but wants to believe he's just being a big brother, protecting her, trying to control her life and her lovers even from his posh Soho apartment in the Big City. She wishes now that she had never confided in him, but the last week had been so horrible, so humiliating she had broken down right in front of him.

"Come and stay with me for a while," her brother had said, as she was crying across the table from him in a new fancy bistro in the middle of Port of Spain. She couldn't stop the tears even when the waiter brought the meal, but her brother didn't look even slightly embarrassed. He poured her some water and said, "Come up and let me take care of you for a while."

She reminded him about her writing course; he was sorry, he hadn't remembered she was doing this. She was irritated because he never remembered her writing, had never really taken her writing seriously. There were no writers, no artists in the family; the family business was business. Her father was the only one who encouraged her, told her to do what made her happy.

"Yes, but you can write anywhere can't you?"

"It's a course, face-to-face, live humans..."

"I never understand how you teach writing."

"You don't teach... It's more like a... never mind."

End of conversation. Her higher self knew he meant well, but right then and there he was upsetting her. He called later that night, after his flight to New York: "Remember what we spoke about, Debs." He has never called her Debbie, like her mother did, or Deborah, like her father, always Debs, "Don't go back. That jackass is no good."

Back in her apartment she isn't hungry anymore, just wants to crawl into bed. The call wasn't his; the text was from the telephone company offering her more deals. Why won't she give this up? The jackass is fine without her, absolutely fine – and not alone. Probably with that little bitch from the office. And this depression thing, this frigging crying all the time is so tiring, so boring. It's been three weeks since she moved out and nothing. She has not heard from him, will not hear from him. He has moved on. Last week she thought she spotted him with that skinny office bitch around the Savannah stopping for coconut water, but it wasn't him, or the skinny bitch.

★

Nights are bad enough, but the day, the day is worse. She hates it when she has to face everyone and say something to them, something that does not give away how awful she feels. Up until last Saturday, she'd worked for a lady selling soap on a stall at a place called The Market – artisan kind of stuff. At her yoga class, a friend had told her that this lady needed someone to work on the stall. So, for the past three Saturdays, she'd found herself selling organic this and that, or talking to an Italian-Trinidadian couple who make pesto from everything besides basil. But then last Saturday she arrived late, and because of her stale drunken state, or because the owner looked a little irritated at her for being forty minutes late, she decided to quit. She told the owner that she didn't want to work for her anymore. "Who the hell is going to pay sixty frigging dollars for a bar of soap? No offence, I mean I get the local, organic, artisan thing, but it's just soap in the end, just frigging soap that you can buy for ten dollars in the grocery." And it was a pittance she was being paid, barely enough to buy a chicken roti and a Coke for lunch. The owner reminded her that she was working on commission and that she had only sold three bars of soap in three weeks. That was the end of that. A dead end if there ever was one. The owner had to be one of the calmest people she had ever met – it had nothing to do with the owner being Rastafarian, the woman was just zen – and Ms Zen had handed her a blue hundred dollar bill and told her thank you.

So no more pushing soap on Saturday mornings, even though she hadn't really pushed any to anyone. But it meant another empty day to get through. It wasn't the money; she had money, though sometimes she pretended to her friends – who really didn't have any money – that she was as broke as they were, but she wasn't broke, she just lived like she was – a kind of broke-writer image. She had inherited money from the sale of two family properties in Tobago. Her brother had asked her if she wanted to invest in stocks, he could tell her which ones; even the local stock market would be better than just putting the money under her bed – though this was exactly where she would have liked to put it. And even though the rates at the bank were a joke, she still was able to add the interest to the money she got from their parents who had passed away within a year of each other.

When they were children she had made a pact with her brother that they would never sell their family home. They had loved it so much, but over last few years, caring for ailing parents had cleared out much of the good childhood memories, and so when their father followed their mother they decided to sell. Her brother lost to the son who couldn't walk into a house that now only reminded him of what was no longer there. Time. All this talk about how precious it was. Time was a frigging curse, time on her hands and nothing to do before the end of August, when she would go back to the private school where she taught art to five-year-olds. These children had imaginations beyond what she could ever teach them.

★

1:00, 1:20, 2:23, 3:15, 5:30, 6 and so it goes, darkness to dawn. Close eyes, open eyes, see red eyes of clock, monster clock, with the numbers looking back. Get up, walk around, go to bathroom, back to bed, lie down, close eyes and try to remember when was the last sleeping pill? 11? 12? Or was it when she turned off the television at 10:45 hoping, even praying, for one night, just one frigging night of unbroken sleep. Insomnia, restlessness, wakefulness, sleeplessness – all of that. But she was suffering from "lostfulness" – that should be a word, she'd coin it. She was sure that there were many others who suffered from the same malady. One night, or two, even three would have been fine; she had never slept well even when he was next to her, even when he massaged her naked body from head to toe with his magical hands. Frigging obeah, he'd put a frigging curse on her so she would never find another peaceful night of sweet sleep. The pills sometimes gave her a couple of hours, but it was never a good sleep; she would always get up groggy. At least the nightmares had stopped. After he left her, the worst night was not first, or the second but the third. That night alone in the new apartment, and without her girlfriends for comfort, she tried to fall asleep after a few glasses of wine, then two shots of Grey Goose – on the recommendation via text of her best friend. Blame it on the vodka. In the dream, they were in their old family home; she was on her parent's huge bed when she heard her brother calling for her to come and help him. She got up quickly and went to the door to find her brother stooping on the landing. He looked stunned and scared and kept saying he didn't know what had happened. She looked closer and tried to reach out to help him to get up when she realized that his arms were just stumps and part of his legs were missing as well, cut off at the knees. Worst of all, the severed parts, arms and legs, were by his side. Her brother's face was terrified and completely confused.

★

In her creative writing workshop there is a king; he is the only published writer in the class, print published, not some obscure internet poetry site, as he reminds the group almost every week. He has written one novel with another on the way. He is a genius who feels he should be leading the workshop, not taking it. He is always trying to impress their creative writing teacher, an African-American prize-winning novelist who has long braids and skin that smells of coco butter. She was once on the Oprah Winfrey show when the Oprah book club thing was hot. With the rest of them, she is not easily impressed, but she praises the King constantly; evidently he intimidates her, too.

The King makes fun of anyone he considers inferior and that is the entire class. Today is her turn. She makes a comment about his story that is not completely gushing with praise. "Great idea Deborah," the King says, "I'll really consider it." His sarcastic tone brings little snickers from the rest of the group and the teacher gives no support to the idea. "Hah, hah, hah," is what she hears, loud laughter confirming that she should not be there, confirming that she is an imposter. She wants to say *Fuck you all!* but instead manages a quick smile, pretending she is not wounded.

At lunch time some of the class sit on a bench near to the house, one or two others occupy the beach chairs facing the sea. There is a low white picket fence and coconut trees along the ridge before the sudden drop down to the water. On one side of the large garden, steps take you to a private bay. Usually she sits on the bench with some of the others, but today she walks down the steps to the bay. No one is there. Before she gets to the last step she stops and sits; the step feels damp on her bare thighs. She is wearing shorts today.

The workshop includes lunch but she usually buys her own, either two doubles from her favourite vendor in town, or she stops at one of the food huts at Maracas Bay for a shark and bake or a bake and cheese. Most of the students sleep at the house where the workshop is being held, but she prefers to drive in every day, even though it takes her an hour from her new apartment.

Alone in her apartment again, she hears the King's comment, the students' snickering, and the silence of the tutor; she decides that the workshop is a waste of time. She cannot face that class again; it is time to stop the workshop. The writing she should have stopped a long time ago.

★

The next day, Sunday, she decides to go to cemetery where her parents are buried. She wants to put flowers on the two graves. No flower shops are open on Sundays so she stops at the neighbour's house with the bougainvillea fence and quickly breaks off a branch. Her brother visited the family plot when he was home a few weeks ago. She'd promised to go with him but at the last minute had chickened out. She has only been to the cemetery twice, once for her mother and three years later to bury her father.

At the cemetery entrance there is a thin old man in an old shirt and faded shorts sitting on the ground next to the gate. His head is bowed and she cannot see his face. After she passes him she looks in the rear-view mirror; the old man has disappeared, another ghost. As she gets closer to the row in the cemetery where her parents are buried she turns around and carries the withering bougainvillea back home.

★

Two months have passed since the workshop; she never went back after that awful day. She knows now that this is where she belongs, teaching primary school art, in front of a class of smiling, non-judging faces. Here she can be the queen, here she can reign and there is Bella in the front row. Bella is her favourite student. Bella is not beautiful; her parents should never have set her up in that way. Bella could even be considered freakish by some: thin red hair, brown skin, light purple-blue eyes and a nose that disappears into her face leaving two small holes. But she adores Bella for her freakishness and the way she looks at her in class, always seeking guidance. Bella believes in her. Bella stand, Bella sit, Bella put red here, blue there, paint a sunflower, and Bella does it, never gives trouble, and does as she is told. She was never like Bella. Her parents could always count on her brother, not always on her. They tried their best not to show their disappointment but she knew she had let them down so many times. Her parents, a being with four hands, four eyes, two heads, speaking with a strange singular voice. She knew they had died worrying about her.

★

Her father had asked her if she wanted anything from him. He did not mean money or land, those things had been taken care of when her mother died. No, her father meant more personal things. Her brother had asked him for a family photograph of them on their first trip to New York. They were all standing outside a hotel, her brother was only nine, she, barely seven. She asked her father for his watch. It wasn't really what she wanted, she only asked for the watch to remember his hands, the hands that had told so many stories, had made her laugh with tickles, had sent her to her room, had slapped her for being rude, had hugged her, hugged them all, the hands that had commanded and carried the weight of the house. Synecdoche. A part for the whole, the sail for the ship, the hand for the father?

★

"How you holding up, Debs?"

"Really good."

"So when you coming up?"

"The term started. I'll see when I can run away."

"My treat."

"I have the money; it's the time."

"Okay, I'll call again soon. Sure you're fine?"

"Yes. Stop nagging; I'm good. I'm over the bad part, okay, not to worry. I'm not about to hang myself from the ceiling. Been there, done that."

"Really not funny, but okay, okay. I'll talk to you soon. Take care of yourself."

"Stop worrying. Love you too, bye."

★

Coconut water and dark rum, his favourite drink; a strapless black thing, his favourite dress. She clears the sofa, makes the bed, cleans the bathroom, sprays on perfume, drinks a glass of white wine after a shot of tequila. He should be here soon. Thank God he finally called.

CHER AMI

They were on a hike, the path down treacherous. At certain points they had to slide on their bottoms to avoid falling over the edge of the cliff; sometimes they had to swing on vines like monkeys. Thank God Zeus was there to help them. He went first, clearing their way with his machete, in his tall black rubber boots, barebacked, loose surfer shorts. He was always steady; he walked as though it were a paved road. Monica was next, dressed as for an aerobics class, then Carolyn, same outfit as Monica, only in brighter colours and finally Baba, in a torn brown T-shirt, washed out black shorts, old sneakers and the widest smile of all.

"When people look at them, I don't really know what they see, but I see my whole life, right there with them. My father had them, his father had them, family tradition, family business, you know what I mean."

Baba was talking about his pigeons; apart from his son, Baba's life was devoted to his pigeons.

"They saved a lot of lives, you know. Look, in World War 1, one of them, a pigeon called Cher Ami, was awarded the "Croix de Guerre", a big prize; wounded and still managed to deliver a message that saved two hundred American soldiers."

"That's amazing," Monica said. She was the only one who was interested; new to the group, she had never heard Baba talk about his birds before. Zeus and Carolyn, or Caro, as Baba always called her, had heard the story many times.

"This is the hardest part and then it gets easy." Zeus didn't turn around when he said this, and the other three just laughed and moaned; every part had been hard from the moment they started.

"Zeus boy, if I knew how hard this thing was going to be, not sure I would have brought these ladies."

"I'm no lady," Caro said, "I can assure you of that."

"Speak for yourself." But the moment Monica spoke, as if on cue, she slipped and landed, very unladylike, with her legs spreadeagled. They all laughed, including Monica.

"You see, the man up there doh like it when you tell untruths." Baba chuckled at his own gibe and helped Monica stand up, even though it meant grabbing onto a thorny tree trunk.

"Watch out for prickers. Don't worry, the rest of the way is not as bad. Soon we'll see the first waterfall. It's a small one now, a little trickle, but in the rainy season you get real water, pouring down like mad."

"How many waterfalls are there?"

★

In the car on the way to the hike, Carolyn had given Monica the rundown on Zeus.

"Zeus is a twin you know, his brother is – was – called Pollo."

"Really, as in chicken? In Spanish, you know, *pollo*." Monica put on her best Spanish accent.

"Such a comedian; no, fool, short for Apollo."

"These are real names?" Monica laughed, but Carolyn said "yes" with a serious face. She had not given it a second thought when she was growing up with them.

"You don't understand. Zeus and Pollo were identical twins; you could barely tell them apart. The one difference was that Pollo had smaller eyes, or different shaped eyes, but listen, they were like gods, brown all over and sprinkled with some kind of gold dust. The girls would just stare at them or turn away, as though the brothers would hold them in some spell; it was funny, weird."

"It gets better. Gods *and* gold dust?" Monica was having fun now.

"Their mother is Dutch or Danish, or something like that, and the father is local. The twins were stars in high school, golden, athletic, on the football team and not stupid – not brilliant either, but certainly not stupid, like some of the others. When you saw Zeus you saw Pollo; it was like that, as though they were somehow still attached."

By now they were driving along the ridge and Monica asked Carolyn to stop so she could take some photographs. From the ridge, you could see the sea on one side and the valley on the other. It was early morning, fresh, and the cool breeze brought with it the smells of chive and dill farmed on the steep hillsides. Monica had not been there since she moved away to Florida with her parents. She was eighteen then.

It was only when she was back in the car and nearly at the spot further up the hill where they were going to meet Zeus and Baba that Monica realized that Carolyn had used the past tense.

"You said he *was* called?"

"What? Who was called?"

"Pollo, Pollo *was* called?"

"Just caught that, did you? You'll see Zeus has a scar on his chin – that's from the accident. Pollo died in a car crash. They were coming back from a party down south, early morning, Zeus, Pollo and two other guys. The one driving – I only remember his last name now, something Laguerre. Anyway, he fell asleep at the wheel and that was it; they crashed into another car after hitting something. Their car apparently flew up in the air and ended up on the other side of the highway, heading back down south instead of facing north. Pollo and the other guy died – damn it, I can't remember his name now. Zeus and Laguerre survived."

"How old was he?"

"Who, Zeus or Laguerre?"

"Yes, Zeus or Pollo, how old are they, were they, was Pollo?"

"I think he must have been in his early twenties, twenty-two or twenty-three."

"Long time ago."

"Not for Zeus. Twenty years for us, two minutes for him."

"So I shouldn't say anything about a brother."

"No, Zeus actually likes to talk about Pollo, at least now. There was a time when he was just lost, left home, disappeared for weeks, months; the parents thought they'd lost two sons."

★

The last waterfall was the least disappointing of the three that Zeus had promised. It actually had water flowing down into a small pond.

"If we had more time we could have taken a little dip; the water is really nice, fresh and cool."

"If we had enough time we could skinny dip; what you think Baba?"

Carolyn loved to tease and flirt with Baba; she knew he'd had a crush on her in their high school days. She'd always been flattered, but never given him much hope. Then, much to her surprise, he married her best friend. Still, life had taken a strange turn; she and Baba were both divorcées now and it was she, not Baba, who was doing the chasing, though she would never admit this.

They could smell the sea on the last part of the hike.

"This is a little tricky," Zeus said, and stopped to make sure they were right behind him.

For the first time since they had started their hike Zeus

looked concerned. The descent had suddenly become steeper. He told them to grip the edges of the jagged rocks, look for spaces and cracks. Now, they were almost at the end of the hike and could see glimpses of the sea through the spaces dense with brush and trees. Zeus gave them a choice: either they could jump from the rock where they were standing into a small pool and swim across to the beach, or continue to climb across the rocks until they got to the bottom of the hill. Baba jumped in and swam across the dark pool, but Monica and Carolyn followed Zeus. With the cutlass now secured in his leather belt, Zeus helped Carolyn and Monica manoeuvre the tricky path. For the first time Monica was afraid that they would not make it; she imagined falling into the pool and hitting her head on a rock. She stopped for a moment, but Zeus held her hand and told her where to put her feet. Carolyn was so athletic she had managed to get to the other side almost in time to meet Baba.

They were all standing on the beach now. The sand was warm, the water a dark green; the bright light was almost a surprise after being so long under the thickly woven canopy of giant trees. It was when they walked closer to the sea that Monica saw the statue. The broken figure of a saint seemed to rise up from the sand and tower above them.

"Which saint is that?" Monica asked

"I think it's Saint Nicholas, to protect sailors, but to be honest I'm not sure," Zeus replied.

"How on earth did it get here? And when?" Monica fascinated, kept walking around the figure of the saint in the middle of the beach. On the way down the others had boasted about the secret beach, but no one had ever mentioned the statue. Zeus told her what he had learnt from one of the villagers, and how he too had been mesmerized by the statue the first time he saw it as a young boy. Monica was happy, even charmed that Zeus had shared this with her – a god who loved a saint. Carolyn was already in the water, telling her to come in. Baba had walked away from them and sat on a log further down the beach. With socks and sneakers in either hand he walked to the edge of the water to wash off the sand and pebbles from the river.

Carolyn's head was bobbing up and down; she had swum out quite far now. The water was mostly calm and flat like a smooth silk sheet, with a gentle wave coming in now and then. Zeus sat on the sand, his boots and cutlass at his side; he was staring at something towards the horizon. Eventually he walked over to Baba.

"They've been friends forever." Carolyn was sitting on the sand next to Monica; she wanted to dry off in the midday sun before putting back on her gym clothes. Carolyn was in such good shape it made Monica feel a little self-conscious.

"I bet Baba is talking about his pigeons and Zeus about the land he wants to sell."

"Does Zeus really live in that hut we saw?"

"Since about a year and a half ago. He's really into being on the land now, growing stuff, selling the property he got from his grandfather. They own a lot of land around here but never really had the money to do anything with it."

"Does he have any children?"

"Who, Baba?" Carolyn turned towards her.

"No, Zeus I mean." Monica looked straight ahead.

"Aren't we very interested now?"

Monica knew Carolyn was deliberately trying to make her feel self-conscious, but said nothing.

"No kids, but his wife left him years ago. You might remember her, she was in a class below us – Michelle Chan."

"Maybe; the name rings a bell… Why did she leave?" Monica had no idea who Michelle Chan was; she just wanted to know more about Zeus.

"Not sure. Maybe Zeus got married too soon after Pollo

died; he was still a mess, so the marriage was a mess. I don't think he ever recovered, I'm not sure he ever will."

"It's hard. I can't imagine losing my sister."

"How is your sister?"

Carolyn and Monica hadn't noticed that Baba and Zeus had climbed up and jumped off a rock at the other end of the beach. They swam over to where the women were sitting, and Baba urged them to come in.

"I swam already," Carolyn shouted.

"So what, you only allowed one swim?"

But then Carolyn got up and walked into the water with her toned body. Monica stayed sitting on the sand. She wished she had the courage to strip down to the bikini she had on under her gym pants and top. She wished she had a morsel of Carolyn's confidence – or was she just too shy to undress in front of Zeus?

Monica watched them, then walked around the statue and tried to read what was written at the base, but what was left of the faded lettering was written in Latin.

The women had packed a few snacks: granola bars, cashew nuts, cranberries – things they had stuffed into Baba's knapsack. Zeus had found two mangoes on the trail so they ate those too as they sat on the sand and chatted about nothing and everything: Baba's desire to visit the Smithsonian one day where the one-legged body of the famous Cher Ami was on display; Carolyn spoke about her bucket list; Monica didn't say how much she hated the expression "bucket list" – the way Americans could make every idea, even death, sound so banal; Zeus spoke about how difficult it was to sell land these days, especially to foreigners who were getting nervous about crime; what had once seemed exotic was now just dangerous. The talk made Monica feel as though she was back home for the first time, even though she had arrived six months ago.

"We'll need to head up soon." Zeus was the first to stand and he held out his hand to pull up Monica and then Carolyn. They dusted off sand and Baba put back on his socks and sneakers he'd been drying on a rock in the sun; Carolyn was already dressed and ready to go. She asked them to pose for a picture, the first with the sea in the background, the second in front of the statue. Monica traded places so Carolyn could get into the photo.

As they started the climb up they chatted about the old days, high school, parties, drinking, smoking. They laughed as Baba reminded Caro about the night she fell asleep on a bench on the savannah.

"In those days that could happen and you could wake up still alive and in one piece," Carolyn said. Monica had little to say, having left for university a month after she finished her 'A' levels. Zeus was silent too, but he laughed at Baba's jokes. Baba talked again about his birds, Zeus about his land. He had got many inquiries, especially about the spot near to the waterfalls, but there had been no down payments, nothing firm and he needed the money badly. Pollo would have told him what to do; that was how it used to be between them. Sometimes the honesty they had with each other could be painful, but at least he knew that whatever Pollo told him was the truth. It was for this he missed his brother most; Pollo was his best friend, his other self. As she listened, taking step after step up the winding hill, Monica wanted to turn around to look at Zeus. When Baba suggested they stop to collect some mangoes on the path, Monica let Baba go ahead of her with Carolyn, but Zeus would not let her walk beside him; he wanted to be last to make sure they were okay. He didn't say much to her as they climbed, but as they got closer to the top where the brush began to clear and they could see the light again, he held Monica's waist to prevent her from slipping. His hand on her body sent a shiver, like a current through her spine, something she had not felt in a long time. She thanked him for the help but he didn't reply. He might have nodded but she couldn't tell.

At the top of the hill, they met other hikers about to make their way down to the beach. They told them about the calm water and the mangoes they might find on their way down. Zeus told them about another route that was a little steeper but at least they would see the waterfalls. The hikers politely declined, preferring to stay on the path they knew.

Carolyn invited Zeus to join them for lunch; they were going to drive down the hill to Maracas beach for shark and bake. Zeus said he wanted to get back home, he had work to do on the land. Baba patted Zeus's back, Carolyn gave Zeus a quick peck on the cheek and Monica said thanks and shook his hand.

★

Almost six months passed before Monica saw Zeus again. She had thought about him, their hike and even the statue of the saint many times. It was in a coffee house in a mall, she was going over something on her laptop for work when he walked in. Monica stared at him, recognising the beautiful face, but not the clothes. Zeus was in a suit and tie. They did not fit well, the jacket looked too lose and not squared at the shoulders, the tie old and outdated. It looked like a suit he might have worn to a wedding or maybe even a funeral; it was heavy and black. He hadn't noticed her so she called out to him.

"Hey Zeus!" she said.

When he turned and saw her, his smile was wide. He came straight across to her table without ordering.

"Haven't seen you in so long, not since the hike, I think. In fact I haven't seen that much of Carole either. We had lunch a couple of weeks ago, but that was it. How are you doing? I like the suit."

Zeus looked immediately embarrassed and Monica was sorry she had mentioned it. She was talking too fast, without thinking, words were just flowing out – it always happened when she was nervous.

"Yeah, I had a meeting at the bank today. I'm okay, I'm good in fact. The big lot, next to the waterfalls, I sold it just in time."

He might have told her that an Englishman bought it, the Englishman might have been a writer, or a painter, definitely an artist of some kind, but she wasn't sure. What she remembered, months after, as she sat on the small wooden veranda in Zeus's hut, was on the day that Zeus walked into that café, despite the embarrassing suit, the gods were finally smiling down on them.

STUFF

There it was again, in the hallway. It had to be coming from the ceiling because she had searched everywhere else; it had to be something up there. Then, in the washroom downstairs she smelt it again. The room was packed with all of their stuff, stuff they needed, stuff they didn't, stuff they should have got rid of years ago but simply couldn't. Now it was as though the foul odour was following her from room to room. Three days now and she could not find its source. Dead lizard, dead frog, or God forbid a dead snake; she had seen one crawl onto the porch and then disappear behind one of the large potted plants. How could a smell, even a dead smell move around a house like that? When she told him this, he looked at her as though she had gone mad. Worse, when he followed her to the place where she had last smelt it, it had moved on to some other part of the house.

She asked him whether he smelt something dead. His "no" was not rebuke, but more like a plea, begging her to stop chasing something that wasn't there. And she wanted to, she was sick of it, but it was there, it wasn't her imagination. You can't imagine a smell, she told him, but the look he gave her said she of all people could.

In the morning, they would leave for work in the dark. She owned a boutique in the mall close to where he worked as a draftsman in an architectural firm. The one car situation was making life a little difficult, but that was all they could afford now; they had even decided to wait before trying for another baby. A baby costs money, he had said. That was not the only reason, and they both knew it, but neither said anything more about it.

The house did not really belong to them; at least that was how she felt, even though she had inherited it from an adored spinster aunt. Before they were married and still living together in a tiny apartment in Cascade she had imagined them buying a new home, a bigger one, like the houses just up the street. Then again, she had also imagined another life to the one she had now and this bothered her more and more as time passed. Her aunt had died quickly; the cancer was aggressive and her aunt never liked a fight. There was no-one exept herself and a nephew in Toronto whohad no intention of moving back to Trinidad, so she had inherited a house that she never really wanted. It was not the house she had dreamed about. They had been living there now for three years since her aunt had crossed over to the other side. That was the way they spoke about it in her aunt's Pentecostal church. She preferred the word dead, disliked those terms that tried to hide the emptiness and silence after the person had gone.

She thought about the smell at work. She told her Venezuelan assistant about it.

"Sometimes, spirits stay and you can smell them," the assistant said. "Sometimes when someone dies you still smell them."

"My aunt died three years ago. Why would I smell her now? It's a rotting smell…" but before she could say *like something dead*, she saw the look of satisfaction on her assistant's face. She said nothing, but reflected that people complicated their lives with silly things. But the next morning, when she thought she smelt it again at the top of the stairs, she remembered what her assistant had said. This time she said nothing to him.

They had not made love in six weeks. She was counting. In the beginning she was the one making the excuses – tired, headaches, falling asleep before he came to bed. Now that he had stopped trying to touch her she was worried. She wanted another baby, she wanted to try again. She was ready. Maybe he was not, maybe he had found someone else, a little less obsessed, someone who didn't wake him up every day asking crazy questions about a smell, someone who was just a little less anxious about life in general.

Then, one morning, she woke up and the smell was gone. Just like that, in the same way that it had entered the house. At first she walked through the house cautiously, warily, afraid that it would return. One morning, once before, it seemed as though it had left the house, but by evening it was there, in another room.

This time she said nothing. The evening passed but she waited a second day just to be sure. On the second morning, she smelled the rain falling in the darkness, she saw the sun rise and the leaves glistening just outside the kitchen window. In that moment just before the dawn, she felt as though a clearing was opening in her mind, a place that could be filled with other things, things that did not weigh her down. That night he must have sensed that she had found that place and when he turned towards her and kissed the back of her neck softly, gently, she took his hand and put it on her stomach, ready to let go, ready to let him in.

ASHES

It had been a long day. I had just got home and was lying on a
sofa on the veranda. Everything was complete now, the final
payment made to the lawyer. Everything so easy. The secretary
had handed me the documents and carefully explained the next
step. I had handed over the cheque; she examined it politely,
with a cursory glance, assuring me that I was trustworthy, that
it was fine. But all the while I'd been hoping that there would
be a fault somewhere, something to cause a further delay, give
me just a little more time. The last documents had been handed
over with a gentle smile and a Manilla envelope.

"Could you sign here please?"

"Is that it?" I asked.

"Yes that's it," she said.

A divorce is like a death, my good friend Sarah said to me; you
grieve. But the difference from a real death? She had no advice
there. She was going through one kind of death, her divorce,
while I was living through another. I was telling her about my
morning, signing the final papers for my aunt's will. I was her
sole executor; my Aunt Claire had never married, nor had any
children. A spinster was what they called women like my dear
old aunt; I hated the word. It made her sound frigid, unwanted,
having led a life without meaning with neither husband nor
child as evidence. I could only hope that word "spinster" would
die a natural death, like my aunt. Dying at 92 had given her a

a good innings, as she would have said – she loved cricket. Sarah hadn't known my aunt well, but remembered how kind she was to us every time we went to her house. The talk of death made us remember a common friend who had lost her eighteen year old son to a car accident.

"How do you get out of bed after that?" Sarah asked.

"Especially if that was your only child," I added. The lights would have gone out with him; my world would be at an end. These were thoughts; I couldn't say the words.

We were having afternoon tea with tiers of cucumber and smoked salmon sandwiches, scones, strawberry compote, clotted cream, and small sponge cakes. The waitress left a handsome wooden box of teas: Darjeeling, Earl Grey, English Breakfast. We both chose Earl Grey. We stayed there until it was dark and they were ready to close their doors. The owner said it was okay for us to stay on a little longer, even though all of the waitresses, save one, had already left. We thanked her but decided to move our little party to a bar not far away. There was still so much to talk about: divorce, sex, death.

It was still early, so there were only a few patrons scattered around. Around seven-thirty or eight the crowd would start to arrive. Sarah ordered a rosé and I got a beer.

"Since when do you drink beer?"

"Since last month. In London that was all I drank, all we drank." I had been travelling with my husband; and that "we" seemed to bother Sarah; her divorce still left a bitter taste.

"If only I had known. How did I not see this coming?" She was looking directly at me when she said this.

"But you didn't know. You were friends. How were you to know that it would turn into what it did?"

I didn't believe what I had said to her and neither did she, but it made us both feel better to pretend that Sarah was the real victim, not the husband whom she had betrayed.

"We were never really happy, you know."

I shook my head as though commiserating, but I didn't buy it. They must have been happy once, because if *they* were only pretending, then all of us were, the entire group of married folk. Something had to be true and Sarah, most of all, had seemed the happiest. Barry adored her and his was no act. When we wives got together and bitched about the bad things our husbands had done to us Sarah could rarely add anything of value. So I couldn't let her continue and changed the topic.

"How is Maya coping?"

"At her age, all she knows is that Mummy and Daddy are now living in separate houses and Uncle Paul is spending a lot more time with Mummy than he used to." Sarah tried to laugh it off, and I smiled too, but it didn't seem very funny. Sarah, even in high school, always seemed to get away with the messes she created: stealing boyfriends, skipping classes, smoking in the bathrooms – nothing seemed to catch up with her, at least not enough to reveal cracks in her beautiful armour.

"We never argue in front of her, we're really very good about that, so I'm not too worried. They say when you get divorced and the kids are young it doesn't affect them as much as if they were teenagers or, you know, more aware of what's happening."

I had no proof of this but I agreed. Sarah needed me to agree.

"When you get divorced, wives don't invite you to their parties anymore. I've been taken off of the list."

"I invite you to all of *my* parties," I said.

"I didn't mean *you*. The others – you know who I mean. I guess they think divorce is contagious – either that or they're afraid that I am about to steal their husbands."

"Or both."

We both laughed. Sarah was beautiful and sexy enough to steal anybody's husband; I kept this thought to myself.

I ordered another beer; she was still nursing her glass of wine. We were both thinking about migrating, so we shared dreams of setting up houses in London, Paris, Barcelona, New York – anywhere but the Caribbean. Sarah felt that Maya should have a better life, more options. I said yes, but didn't wholly agree. The Caribbean was still a good place to raise a child, and we had family and friends to call on in times of need.

"Will Barry let you take her?"

"Probably would put up a fight, but eventually he'd give in."

I think she underestimated the power she still had over him.

I couldn't tell how serious she was about this, although I knew she had always wanted to live abroad. Having married young, Sarah had never had the opportunity, like some of her friends (I was included in that group), to have lived and studied abroad. Maybe now she was ready to go.

"This place can be suffocating," she said.

This time I was in total agreement, "Yes it can be."

"A small place," Sarah said.

I thought immediately of Jamaica Kincaid's book, which I was sure Sarah had not read. She had never been a reader like me.

"You know, like that book." Sarah said.

"What book?" I couldn't believe that Sarah had read any book from cover to cover, far less by a writer like Jamaica Kincaid, or even knew who Kincaid was for that matter.

"By that Jamaica woman."

"Jamaican you mean?" I was now deliberately trying to throw her off track.

"No, her *name* is Jamaica."

"Oh, you mean Jamaica Kincaid."

Of course. She always got names wrong, she laughed.

"We all do," I said condescendingly, but Sarah didn't seem to notice the tone.

We stayed a little longer, watched as the crowd began to
come in, all dressed for an evening lime at a posh drinking hole.
Sarah and I were still in our tea clothes, lighter colours as
opposed to the black now filling the place. We recognised a few
faces, said a quick "Hi", then "Goodbye".

By the time I got home I was in a cloudy, uneasy state. On
the sofa I kept replaying the Kincaid thing in my mind. How
could she have known about Kincaid's *A Small Place*? It had to
have been Paul's influence, but I had never heard him refer to
one single writer or book in the many years since I'd known
him. And Sarah didn't even look as unhappy as I thought she
would have, or should have. In fact, Sarah looked as though she
had finally found the man of her dreams. In Paul of all people.
Sarah was happy and she was free. Somehow she had won
again, the way Sarah always had since our high school days, in
a race that she didn't even know she was running.

A neighbour was burning some rubbish in their yard. I
noticed how sometimes leaves were falling from a nearby tree,
and sometimes ashes would just appear in the air, wriggling
like black worms.

TAP TAP

In the customs line I overhear American accents behind me; they are here for the conference where the writer I am here to interview is going to read from her new work on Haiti and lead a plenary session. This time I have no embassy help, so I have to line up with everyone else, get all my documents ready and prepare for the questions at customs. There are a few other Caribbeans in the line with me, but only one other journalist, working for my old newspaper. He doesn't recognise me but I remember when he came in as a new entry to the office, ready to start his career just as I was preparing to leave. I had spotted him before we boarded in Miami. He stood out because he was trying so hard to fit in, talking as much French as he could. His French seemed good enough but his overenthusiasm and incessant prattling made me want to knock him out for at least a few minutes – though my ex-colleague seemed so happily superior to the rest of us monolingual mortals that he barely noticed me glaring at him. I was grateful that I didn't see much of him again after that first day at the airport, and I am quite sure he quickly sized up our group and realized that there was little to be gained here; we were not high enough on his ladder to fulfil whatever ambitions he had.

As I walked through the airport I felt faint and could barely breathe. It was hot, thick, and noisy. Had taking this assignment been my best plan? But I was due some success. I had resigned from my last job when it became clear that my face did not fit. The truth was not everyone was being laid off, only two full-time staff members were on that restructuring list, me and another journalist from the sports section of the daily, though this was not the impression I allowed anyone who asked to gather, especially to my boyfriend. Freelancing now, I was able to get this small gig because my boyfriend's father knew the managing editor of a travel magazine. I was hoping that this interview would help me get, if not a permanent job with the magazine, at least a few more articles.

I had never met my writer before, barely knew her work; my BA was in English–American Literature, not Caribbean. But I studied her bio on line, looked at a few of her interviews on YouTube and almost finished her first book. In my humble opinion what I read was good, not great, but certainly not genius. My writer hadn't been particularly forthcoming in responding to the questions I had sent to her in my emails. Although her responses were sent in a timely fashion, usually within a day or two (not typical for the other writers and artists that I had interviewed) they were short, and precise, never warm, but also not impolite. Her email style was completely unlike the long, winding almost Conrad-like sentences that had made her so famous. In fact the prize that she had just won even mentioned her complex syntax. To most of my questions my writer suggested that we could "discuss all of this further in Haiti." In recent photographs of her at various events, and on YouTube (I paid particularly close attention to the recent award-winning event in New York) she looked pleasant, smiling, even easy going. But my research on the interviews that she had given never offered much information; that was part of her mystique. All the acclaim she'd received was not unusual for a young writer – getting into a first-rate publishing house was also not completely uncommon, but she had never been to any famous creative writing programmes, had no patron writers to help her out, just a "good agent", she had said. She was of Caribbean origin on her father's side, her mother was British. She'd been raised in the Caribbean, the UK and the US, majored in psychology with a minor in literature. Her father was an engineer, her mother a homemaker. According to my writer, she was just "one of the lucky ones." I didn't believe in luck.

★

"They say patience is virtue and virtue is grace." These were the words of the man who sat next to me on the tap tap, oldish, seventyish I guessed, with an Irish accent and bright pink, rumpled skin and tea-coloured teeth. Outside the hustlers were still quarrelling over who should get the tips for putting our luggage on the top of the bus. The noise from the men was so loud I thought that there would be a fight to the death for a few gourdes, or a bounty of two US dollars. Soon the driver, our tap tap hostess and her tout managed to sort out the mess about tips and the bus slowly made its exit through the crowed airport. We looked on but said very little to each other or about the chaos outside. All of the tap taps were covered with art work. There were murals with American, Haitian and other Caribbean flags painted on doors or rear-view mirrors, bumpers were covered in images of lions, tigers, Rastafarian heads, bananas, oranges, "Gods Power", "Africa". No spot was left untouched: greens, reds, oranges, yellows, whites, blues and all the hues in between. We were travelling in a moving painting, on iron seats painted blue, hard on the back and backside. I tried a few times to release the smell of sweat and perfume inside the tap tap but the window would not slide. Brakes were screeching, gears grating, everything suggested pain. This converted camion/ bone crusher was the public transport that I had only seen from my comfortable air-conditioned Prado the last time

I was in Haiti when, real or imagined, the traffic on the roads seemed to part before us like the Red Sea.

Initially we had all admired the painted vans but after crawling in the Port-au-Prince traffic for hours in the early afternoon heat, with other vehicles close enough for the drivers to talk or swear at each other, much of our love for naïve native art was beginning to fade, and this was when the Irish man turned and said, "They say patience is a virtue and virtue is grace." He looked as though he was perishing, probably not used to this punishing weather.

With a grand announcement from our tap tap hostess, we pulled up. We had finally arrived at The American Hotel in Pétion-Ville. Her English was difficult to understand but we caught the words "hotel" and "American". As the driver was about to make a sharp turn into the driveway leading to the hotel, a very serious Haitian guard raised one hand signalling him to stop. We couldn't help but notice that his other hand rested on a big black semi-automatic weapon slung over his shoulder. The guard stood in front of a tall iron gate that was closed. Something was said in Haitian by our driver that must have reassured him because the guard then opened the gates. The guard had yet to say a word, he just shook his head and signalled the driver to enter. As we drove in slowly, we saw a rundown hotel that looked as though parts of it had been destroyed by the 2010 earthquake. Those staying at The American were told that this was our stop. Obediently we got out, very concerned about the location and the stern, unfriendly armed guard. But just as the tout was about to take down our suitcases from the roof of the tap tap, my Irish friend rescued us: "I'm not sure that we are in the right place." He pointed to a sign above the stairs leading to the foyer of the hotel. The driver and hostess insisted that this was the place and paid no attention to the sign or my Irish friend. *Le Papillon,* it said, with decorative, seriffed letters that gave the idea of wings. Only then did we notice the fading mural of many species of butterflies, including the Emperors, painted on the walls. It was easy to miss the sign since the first "P" was covered with overhanging vines, which must once have been a charming arbour over the entrance.

We stared at the sign, transfixed, confused, tired, worried, wondering why the driver and hostess had brought us to the wrong hotel. The American academics looked especially anxious: Had they been brought here to be robbed? Murdered? This was Haiti for Christ's sake, anything was possible.

Then a Jamaican journalist who had been silent for most of the trip realized what we had all missed – the driver had been asking for directions since we got into Pétion-Ville. I began to realise, as did perhaps the rest of my tap tap comrades that the driver was not used to being in this area; private taxis, not tap taps drove guests to the hotels on these hills. And our Jamaican whispered to the rest of us: "I don't think he can read." Indeed, even after we pointed to the sign, the driver still insisted that this was the place and signalled for us to get our luggage out of the vehicle. After much discussion in languages that were not Haitian, nor French, nor English, but a combination of all of these we managed to convince the driver and our tap tap hostess that this was the wrong place and we needed to get in the bus once again. What was even more bizarre was that the guard had never said a word confirming or denying whether this was Le Papillon or The American. He never left his post at the tall iron gates. When we were all back inside the tap tap and the iron gates finally closed behind us, I suddenly felt a rush of adrenalin and my hands began to shake. I put it down to too much coffee and tried to convince myself that the entire situation had not shaken me up – perhaps even more than the Americans.

Back out on the main street we stopped yet again to hear the driver being given more instructions to our hotel. After almost another hour, stopping many more times, we finally walked into the air-conditioned world of The American. The change from outside to inside the modern-looking building was dramatic. We left the frenetic streets to enter a cool, calm world of beautiful Haitian receptionists checking us in and suggesting we go across to the bar for a welcome fruity rum punch. Although we were all beyond exhausted, we stayed at the bar for a while to chat and find humour in the tortuous drive from the airport. Then the group began to break up. The academics said they needed to work on their papers, but I suspected they also didn't want to exceed their travel budgets, except my Irishman who ordered another beer, a local one, and I got another rum punch. I had always preferred to travel with artists and journalists who probably had less disposable cash than the academics, but were willing to spend it much faster. Unfortunately, my writer was not staying at this hotel; the conference organisers had put her up at an undoubtedly more posh location closer to the conference centre. They had probably also provided more comfortable transport.

By the time I got up to my room the rum in the punch had taken effect. I had planned to do some more research on my writer, to send a long WhatsApp to tell my boyfriend about the arrival, the confusion about the hotel and any other funny detail I could think of. Instead, I simply sent: *Arrived safe long trip to hotel lots to tell love you talk soon*. I had taken pictures of the tap tap but didn't bother to send them. After a quick shower to wash away the dusty, sweaty day I fell into a restless sleep until the morning light flowed into my room. I woke up in panic, afraid that I had missed the tap tap pick-up to the conference because I had forgotten to ask when that was supposed to be. The bedside clock said 7:36. I showered quickly and threw on clothes – a pair of jeans, tee-shirt, and jacket – fixed my rumpled face as best as I could with lip gloss and mascara and sprayed on some perfume. Before I grabbed my bag, I checked my phone to see if my boyfriend had sent me a message but I could see that my message hadn't even been read. I tried to brush off the silly feeling of disappointment, thought about sending another message, but stopped myself from looking too needy. Almost forgetting my card for my room I rushed to the receptionist downstairs. She was the same one from the evening before and I wondered whether she had spent the entire night there. She still looked so perfect I felt even more dishevelled. She had no information about the tap tap. I looked around hoping to see someone else from the group. At first, no one, and then there he was again, my Irishman waiting in a chair close to the hotel entrance. He waved, probably noticing my confused look: "Our friends haven't arrived as yet." I smiled back, truly relieved. It was just after eight, according to my friend, that the bus was supposed to be outside the hotel. I decided to go for the beautiful rooftop view where the buffet breakfast was being served. My Irishman promised to keep guard and notify me if the tap tap arrived. I preferred to eat alone, even though I recognised some American academics from the day before. The cheese and mushroom omelette, fresh mango juice and sliced watermelon were delicious and the rich dark Haitian coffee was simply heaven. The morning was bright and everything seemed right with the world from that rooftop restaurant – even if he still hadn't read my message.

The tap tap had lost both novelty and charm by the second day, with the smell of kerosene and petrol, the loud sound from the engine, the hard seats, the heat, the young boys jumping onto the side of the van to hitch a ride and everyone shouting to exchange simple greetings. All of this frenetic activity could

have left me with a stubborn headache, but the day had begun
with a special Caribbean morning light. It was sharp and clear,
like looking out through a freshly cleaned window. This light
reminded me of a poem I loved about a young girl running
across freshly cut grass on a morning like this one. And that
poem reminded me of my childhood when my parents would
take me to the Queen's Park Savannah on Sunday mornings
and let me run wild. It was one of the few vivid memories I still
had of my parents. All of this helped me survive another long
drive through dense, noisy morning traffic.

When we finally crawled into the grounds of the posh conference hotel an hour and a half later, late for the first plenary
session which had started at nine, our tap tap hostess tried to
explain to us slowly and carefully in Haitian, with snippets of
English words and gestures, where we should wait for the bus if
we wanted a ride back to our hotel in the afternoon. Only after
our hostess left with a wide smile and a royal wave did we realize
that although we had all politely nodded our heads, no one was
actually sure about the time and place. We hadn't paid much
attention to her and wrongly assumed that the conference
organisers would fill in the details for us. This confusion was to
come later after a long day of academic papers, plenary sessions,
and an expensive sandwich and Haitian coffee from the hotel
cafeteria. Haitian coffee – my writer had referred to it in her first
book. I added this to my list of things I wanted to discuss when
we met. What was the significance of the coffee? Did it represent
something more profound to her?

For the entire day the hotel lobby was buzzing with all the
people for the conference, most of them seated at the bar. In
fact there was more activity at the bar than there was upstairs
where the papers were being presented. It felt more like a party,
a meet and greet, a long-time-no-see kind of happening rather
than a place for serious intellectual exchange. I was alone at the

area where we could charge our phones; I wanted to send a short message to my editor. The group of academics and others I had come with had found other university colleagues. I had been checking my phone throughout the day for messages or missed calls from my writer and from my boyfriend. There was nothing from both. I did some detective work and found out that my writer had arrived and was in the hotel. Someone had seen her at breakfast, but when the desk called her room there was no answer. We had confirmed, or at least had *said*, in our last email before leaving for Haiti that we would meet at some point during the afternoon of the first day for a coffee and a chat. Either she had forgotten, or was purposely ducking me. Maybe she had gone on some expedition to buy the Haitian art work she so admired. Those were the only options I could come up with at the moment. I sent her an email saying where I was, gave her my hotel room number at The American and asked if we could meet tomorrow if today was impossible for her. I messaged my boyfriend: *Hey, haven't heard from you hope all is well. Second day still no sign of my star girl!!!*

A poetry reading by the pool at three o'clock was open mic and many of the young writers came forward to read their work. There weren't many people listening; I sat along with a few of their friends under the hot tent. A few of the writers were from Haiti; they read in Haitian and one in French. There was another from the Dominican Republic with a voice that was so soft (even with the mic) that the small audience could barely understand what she was saying – the whispering poetess, I named her. I could only understand the ones in English read by a young Jamaican writer with a strong accent and an American who told us he was really Caribbean in spirit and tried his best to mimic a Jamaican accent. I remained untouched by the poems, but poetry was never my thing. Eventually the heat in the tent became unbearable, so I decided to try

yet again to call my writer's room. No writer. The phone rang
and rang again. No reply from my boyfriend.

I went back to the bar and asked a familiar face if she had seen
my writer. She hadn't. No sighting yet and I only had these
three days in Haiti before I had to get back home. To kill some
time I snuck into one of the last plenary sessions for the day, a
discussion on some obscure academic theme followed by even
more obscure questions; buzz words and hip theories flew
through the enlightened air. I was lost, kill-me-now bored and
more than a little irritated. The promise of the bright morning
had not panned out during the day. By five o'clock I was ready
to go back to the hotel, so I waited outside for my tap tap. The
only other member of my group with me was my Irishman; he
looked tired and his face was even redder than before. Although there were a few other tap taps and some luxurious
black taxis at the front of the conference hotel, our ride was
nowhere to be found. A husband and wife couple, both American, came up to us. I barely recognized them from the day
before, but they too were waiting. We stood there for almost an
hour, asking questions every now and then at the conference
desk where the young Haitian volunteers from the conference
were gathered. They had no information on our tap tap
departure time. In fact they didn't seem to know anything at all
about the arrangement with these drivers. Eventually someone
from our group came out to the entrance to let us know that
they were staying on there for an evening event and dinner. My
journalist budget did not include this, so I stood in the front
with my Irishman and two other Caribbean academics and
waited for another hour before an angry tap tap driver, our
own, pulled up at the front of the hotel. The hostess explained
to one of the volunteers that we were supposed to have waited
at the back of the hotel not the front. Apparently they had been
waiting for us for the last two hours. End of day one.

The next day had to be better. We had managed to work out a system with the tap tap hostess; a combination of sign languages and our bad Haitian but it worked. The tap tap arrived only fifteen minutes late the next morning and even the traffic seemed a little better, or perhaps we had all lowered our expectations to the point where anything would have been better than that first day. My night had been spent fighting with my boyfriend, who finally responded saying that he had left his phone in the office. By the time he went back to pick it up he saw eight messages from me. These eight included the first two I had sent, but by the time I had gotten to number five with no response from him, my attempt at sounding casual ended. I imagined him back with his old girlfriend, both of them laughing at me as they lay naked in his bed. My last text was not my best moment: LET ME KNOW NOW IF YOU WANT TO END THIS BECAUSE I AM FUCKING READY TO GO!!!!!! He managed to convince me that his phone was actually in the office and that I needed to remember what my therapist had said about my trust issues. By this time we had stopped sending texts and were trying to talk on the phone, but the connection was very poor. In the end we both felt exhausted, going around in circles, and just hung up.

The next morning I felt ragged so I decided to distract myself by focusing on my mission to find my writer, even if it meant camping at her hotel door. Time was running out on me to get my interview and I basically had one day and a morning before my flight back home via Miami.

My Irishman was also in a sombre mood that morning and although he still managed to smile at me as we got into our bus, there seemed a veil of sadness. I did not want to pry, just asked if he was okay.

"It goes by fast," he said. "I know you hear this a million times, but it does and still we take it all for granted."

"Yes, I guess we do." I had not expected him to be so forthcoming.

"My daughter's father-in-law, gone just like that." He snapped his fingers as he said it and, as though in response, the tap tap stopped suddenly and we all jerked forward.

"Careful." He held my upper arm gently to prevent me from hitting the iron seat in front of us.

But he didn't continue talking and for the rest of the trip to the conference hotel we were silent. Silent as we passed the boy on the street with only one slipper waving down the bus; silent as we passed piles of garbage; silent as we saw the mopeds weave in and out of traffic like flies, skilfully avoiding the crushing wheels of our tap tap. I didn't tell him that death was something I knew well. I had lost both parents to a car accident as a child and had been raised by my grandmother who had passed away only two years ago. Much of my life had been spent learning to live with death.

Just as we were about to turn into the hotel I asked him if he was presenting his paper that day. My Irishman said he was presenting a paper on the work of Jacques Roumain.

"I expect seven people and that includes our panel of four presenters." He managed a chuckle but added that no one was really interested anymore in what he was doing, but he didn't care. "An academic dinosaur is what I am now, soon to be extinct." He laughed at his quip.

"I'll try to make it," I said. He just smiled and we both knew that I was not going to show up.

Unlike the day before, and despite my horrible night, I tried to be calmer about the meeting with my writer. She was supposed to be on a panel for Caribbean writers from the diaspora, so even if she had been avoiding or ignoring the interview with me, she had to appear for this. The room for this panel was packed but I managed to get a seat near the front. My writer had her own following, the room was full to hear her read and to talk with fellow Caribbean writers about the state of the region, its politics and what she called its poetics.

I was quite sure she wouldn't recognize me from my profile pic. I knew now that she had barely paid attention to anything I had sent her. Who was I to her anyway? Some unknown journalist from some unknown Caribbean magazine? Just like my old colleague at the airport, she had put me in the "not worth the effort" basket. Often described as striking, her photos were usually head shots that played up her large, light green, almond-shaped eyes; her hair, a mixture of copper and gold; her light brown skin with yellow undertones and the famous freckles. But the first thing I noted as I approached her was a strong fresh smell of lemons, a scent that seemed to match everything else about her. I had my notes on paper and in my head. In *Freckles,* her first novel (the one I had almost finished) she had written about her mixed Caribbean-British background. It had won her the Commonwealth prize and many more prizes followed soon after. Although she looked thirty-two she was actually forty-two and had already written two more novels after *Freckles*, three collections of short stories, and a book of poetry. She had said in a recent interview that she was working on a screenplay. She was already twice divorced, most recently to a well-known American artist, and before that from a Brazilian architect. Both men were at least twice her age. She had no children.

"Writing shouldn't be martyrdom or even masochism, it shouldn't be romanticized or an excuse for bad behaviour. The hungover café writer is beyond passé." I had heard and read those lines before. She has said it during the days of Oprah's book Club when *Freckles* had been selected as book of the month. She had said it in a New York Times interview, and now she was saying it again here. She was self-plagiarising or perhaps only had this one idea, but no one else seemed to care, the audience nodded. I tried to reset to my more upbeat self and to at least pretend to be excited to be here. Throughout the discussion I kept checking my phone for messages; there was nothing from him. My writer always kept interviews, appearances and readings to a minimum; she would not be seen as chasing fame. This profile suited her well; it left her followers wanting more; so rather than bombard her readers with information, she seduced them with intermittent tweets and a fragments of information and ideas on her web page.

Somehow the magazine had managed to get this interview. Maybe the timing was good, because recently she had been talking about her Caribbean heritage and her screenplay was to be semi-autobiographical, set in Barbados, Grenada, Jamaica and of course, London. This Caribbean conference was a way of underlining her right to write about a place she had left at ten years of age and had only revisited as a woman of thirty. Since then she had come more regularly. "I hate when writers talk about their tragic family background to explain the gifts that they possess, as though creativity and tragedy were indelibly linked, a bad marriage if you ask me." And yet she had hinted at a traumatic episode in her childhood. This was her magic trick: innocence and cynicism combined.

At the poolside, under one of the wide, thatched umbrellas, a Coca-cola for my writer and a coffee for me. I was more nervous than usual, knowing I had to get this right and also because she had an unnerving way of looking directly into my eyes when I asked her a question, or moving forward towards me to reply. She seemed to appreciate all the questions I had prepared about her fame and her roots in the Caribbean. I had emailed all of the possible questions beforehand. I asked nothing about her marriages, or politics, but I did ask about the last book she had written, stating how much I had enjoyed it.

In truth I had never actually read it, I just read the reviews. But to add a little spice to my interview, I mentioned that one critic had basically said that she should stick to prose. The critic's words were of course much more elegant but that was the gist of the criticism. I knew that this might ruffle her a bit, but I felt I needed something more to impress my editor.

"I never saw myself as a poet, or playwright for that matter, it was just a way of exploring other genres, the way painters or musicians are allowed to experiment with different styles. And ultimately I am glad that I was brave enough to try different things." Her tone was still calm and said with a smile, but I could see that she was a little irritated. Something I had also noticed struck me the more we spoke, was that although she was born in Tobago, she sounded neither Caribbean nor English but American. So I asked about her accent and tried to link it to her multiple origins, hybrid identity, her intersectionality (at this point I was trying hard to sound like the academics). Again she looked a little uneasy but responded calmly, saying that she had lived in New York for quite a few years with her last husband and perhaps had acquired a bit of the twang. After that she tried to throw in a few phrases here and there that sounded more Caribbean, but the intonation was never really on point. My last question was about her screenplay. Why did she suddenly want to focus on the Carib-bean and when was her last visit to Tobago? "It was time to come home," she said, and I was pleased that she had given me the closing lines to my piece.

After a few photographs taken with my phone, I thanked her several times for the interview and we promised to stay in touch, although, based on the last few days, I knew I would never hear from her again. In all we had spoken for about an hour including short chats and congrats from passers-by; she never seemed rushed and had it been my last encounter with her my overall impression would not really have changed much from what I originally thought, but she had charm, lots of it, and knew how to use it. When she left I remained sitting at the pool making a few more notes: Sea Island cotton dress, calm measured tone, intensity of stare, compliments from people, rock star persona, etc. During the interview she never called me by my first name, or any name for that matter, and when I said that I would send her a copy of the interview before it went to print she asked me to remind her of the name of the magazine. All this nonchalance was in keeping with the care-free persona she wanted to portray to the world, but I knew that this interview probably didn't matter to her, but at this stage, having hounded her throughout the conference, I was just happy to have it done. The relief was twofold since I finally got a message from my boyfriend saying he was sorry we had fought and couldn't wait for me to get back home. His message ended with two emoji hearts. Life was good again.

My last evening in Haiti was to be spent with a few members of our tap tap brigade, including my Irishman. We had planned on our last morning tap tap trip to the conference to meet at our hotel bar for drinks around 7ish and then go out to dinner at a quaint restaurant within walking distance of our hotel; one of the more adventurous members, a young French PhD gradu-ate student had found the restaurant on her first night in Haiti. I had looked forward to this get-together all day, especially since the interview and text from my significant other. I was feeling light again and unburdened. But I never made it to the bar and for this I blame my writer. Just before heading to the main entrance of the conference hotel to meet our tap tap, ready for my evening of drinks and dinner, I decided to reward myself with a souvenir to remember my trip. I went into a small boutique at the conference hotel where they sold high quality Haitian coffee, wallets, handbags and jewellery – all expertly crafted by local artisans. The Haitians had always had this elegance and artistry. The owner of the boutique, a statuesque woman who spoke perfect English, saw how much I had appreciated the work in the store and invited me to see more handbags that were in the storeroom. These she usually put aside for some of her top clients.

I was about to select one of the bags when I heard a familiar voice in the next room. The shop owner's assistant was showing my writer and another woman some items in the store. They were saying how beautiful everything was and I was about to go out to greet my writer once again when I heard the question:

"So, how did the interview go?"

"Disaster," my writer said.

"Really, why?"

I froze waiting for the response, so much so that the shop owner almost bumped into me as she was about to turn and show me another item.

"The girl had to be an idiot, asking stupid questions about things she could have googled. I really don't know why a magazine would even bother to send someone like that. She obviously hadn't read my work."

"Well, at least you'll get some mileage for the new book?"

"What, in some unknown, crappy magazine? But at least *she* got a free trip."

They both laughed. I couldn't move and I heard myself tell the shop owner that I really didn't see anything I needed. She just smiled graciously and indicated with her bejewelled hand that I re-enter the main room. Luckily I heard a tinkle and the door close behind my writer and her friend.

I was thirty-four, but I felt like crying, not a quiet, discreet, adult cry, but one where curl up in your mother's or grandmother's arms and just bawl. Packing that night all I could hear was my writer's voice saying I was an idiot, saying I asked stupid questions, saying I didn't know her work. I couldn't parse the truth from the fiction. I didn't send a text to him that night.

★

"Duvalier should have never left. When they were here, I can tell you everything was working fine, there was no crime, and you could walk the streets at night."

I didn't bother to reply to my Haitian taxi driver, the owner of a comfortable air-conditioned sedan, on my way to the airport the next morning. He had learned all of his English in high school and on his frequent trips to visit relatives in Miami; his English had a strong American twang. In our discussion up until then we had agreed on the state of Haiti, the corruption, the violence, the devastation before and after the earthquake. Up until then I thought we both understood that everyone was to blame for a crime that had been committed here a long time ago. But I was not Haitian and didn't think I had the right to question even the reign of terror from both father and son. With every bone in my body I disagreed but said nothing, and simply smiled – the same way our tap tap hostess had smiled at us every morning, probably understanding, as I did, a lot more than she wanted to reveal.

★

When I got in my boyfriend was there to meet me at the airport. How did it go? Really well, I said. I managed to write up the interview in a couple of days, sent it to my writer but as expected she never replied but my editor loved it. The only thing he asked me to cut were the rides in the tap tap and my Irishman.

2: STICK NO BILLS

THE AUGUST WARS

At the seaside we are a band of four, me and my three cousins, all girls, a girl band, ready to take on the group of boys living in the house next door. Our parents told us a thousand times not to go down to the beach alone, not to wander around the compound, and never go into the caretaker's house without them; we are not old enough. But in the afternoons, when they are all asleep, taking their naps after too many gin and tonics or rum punches – before, after and sometimes during lunch – we follow through on our secret plans. We all have our names: I am not Lisa but Legs, my older cousin Patty is Cakes, and my two younger cousins, Jennifer and Joanna, are called the Twins even though they do not look alike and are not twins – though when they speak, if your eyes were closed, you wouldn't know one from the other. Cakes and I tell the Twins what to do; they fetch us water, coconut ice cream, and carry most of the supplies we need when we go on hikes down to the beach, or do battle with the boys next door. The Twins follow our commands around the compound; they have no choice. The compound – that's what we all call it – has three houses built by my grandparents for each of their three daughters: Juliette, Isabella and Miranda. All names from plays my grandfather loved. My grandparents live in the main house built for Aunt Miri; this house was the first to be built. Each house looks the same – same number of bedrooms, same number of bathrooms, same long porch looking out to the ocean. The only differences are the movables, people and things. Each house is named after a daughter, so we might say we are going to have dinner at Miranda's, or my mother, Isabella's (although everyone called her Bella) or Juliette's. Bella is the middle daughter; Juliette, the youngest daughter, is the mother of Cakes and the Twins. The eldest is Aunt Miri, married, then divorced, then almost married again. She never had any children although we all think she would have been the best mother of them all. She is the aunt we go to whenever there are fights in the compound, and she is the aunt who can bring light back to us on our grey days.

On this particular Saturday afternoon, the Twins carry water balloons and buckets. We try our best to respect the adult rules but we, meaning Cakes and yours truly, no longer see ourselves as children, especially since we are going to start high school in September. The Twins are children, eight and nine, but we are not. The only adult who understands this is Aunt Miri. She encourages us to explore the compound, tells us that life goes by fast. Before you know it, you are almost at the end, your last chapter, so write your own book, she tells us. At the time those words meant very little to us – all we needed to know was that Aunt Miri was on our side. Still, there is her one golden rule: no lies. If broken, a different Aunt Miri appears, like some multi-headed snake monster. The first time we saw this was when we stole two Cadbury milk chocolate bars from the fridge in the main house. You would have thought that we had stolen golden bars instead of chocolate ones, but we paid the price. You slip, you slide, Aunt Miri said. One lie always leads to another. That was it, banned from the beach for two days.

Bella, my mother, is known to all as the worrier, but according to Aunt Miri, she is not a bad soul, just a worried one. My mother expects a bolt of lightning, a tidal wave, a pack of wild dogs or a crazy person to suddenly appear and attack us at any moment. So we tell my mother as little as possible – for her own good. And then there is my Aunt Juliette, who prefers singing to talking, who lives in a world that no one else can get to, who seldom raises her voice except to call us all to lunch, dinner or tea – so Cakes and the Twins have it really easy. This is why I never speak up if we are caught; Cakes does all of the talking; she has a way of explaining to the adults why we put vinegar into the water bottles, or salt in the sugar bowl, or how a very small fire started under the coconut trees, or why the coconut ice cream disappeared from the freezer, or how sand got into the beds in all three houses. Cakes can talk her way out of anything.

Three boys spend their vacations next to our compound; their land is the same size as ours and their one big house looks as though someone stuck our three together. They are our arch enemies. We hate every bone in their skinny bodies; at least that is what Cakes and I say about the boys to each other. They make us want to break the rules; they taunt and dare us to do things we probably wouldn't otherwise do. Mark, Simon and Paul, the Monkey Boys, are usually armed and ready for our after-noon attacks. The war normally starts around three in the afternoon on the western side of our compound. First there are the small white pebbles that they throw over from their side. We respond in kind, but add a little more dirt and gravel to the mix. Then the boys throw over the green or dry almonds that have fallen to the ground and we throw them back. We have almond stacks on our side as well. These are just the early stages of battle, small signs that tell us to meet them at the front wall of the compound, near to the main gate for the second stage. This is where the real battle begins, the water stage. We line up buckets of water and balloon bombs behind the wall near the main gate; our balloon bombs never fail to hit their mark. The Twins are experts at filling them with just enough water so that they don't burst in our hands before we launch them over the wall.

Normally, before the second stage begins, there is an exchange of warring words: who will crush who, who will cry like little girls, who will run home to their mummy, who looks like a monkey (the boys), who are ugly cockroaches (the girls), and who will die or live to fight another day. The boys normally start the fight because we, meaning me and Cakes, have a strategy. We let them use most of their balloon bombs, we throw just a few and then we really attack. The winner of this stage is the team who throws the last balloon over the gate. I don't think the boys really care who wins they just want to make sure we get soaked.

We can only see each other at our wide gate which is usually padlocked; the Monkey Boys are on the outside, on the road, or hiding behind the wall. Tall cement walls surround our property on all sides except for the sea view where my grandparents put a very low wall to allow what my Grandpa Alex calls "an uninterrupted view of my ocean". Because that part of the ocean belongs to him, he says with his deep laugh that sounds like a cough. Before the Monkey Boys moved in next door, their property was owned by one of Grandpa Alex's oldest friends, a man we all called Uncle Joey, or the Mighty Joe as he was known in the village. The Mighty Joe loved the sea, a good rum punch, a game of All Fours and my grandmother's bouillon. The Mighty Joe was my grandpa's best friend. After he died the Monkey Boys' parents bought the property and named it Notre Paradis. Grandpa Alex said it was a show-off kind of name, and he didn't like the neighbours either, even though they had never done anything to us. In fact, every time they came up to the seaside, their mother and father brought us mangoes, avocadoes or sometimes sweet bread that the mother had baked. Granny, accepted all of their gifts graciously and often returned the favour with her own sponge cake and banana bread. It was good to be neighbourly she would say, but Grandpa's grumpy mood never changed with them. Maybe he thought it would make him disloyal to his old friend or maybe he was just annoyed that his partner in crime had left him. None of this meant too much to us. We, meaning Cakes, the Twins and I, call this time the August Wars, when the Monkey Boys and their family were at the seaside, like us, for the month of August.

CAMPING

Sometimes, if we behave well, they let us camp outside overnight. We do this with our fathers. My father, unlike my mother, is no worrier, and camping is one of his favourite things to do when we are at the seaside. He is the one who encourages the other adults to let us sleep outside, even though my mother worries about snakes, catching cold, and tarantulas. Usually we camp quite near to the main house because it is cooler and windier at night and we are closer to the ocean. Two tents are set up very near to each other and we try our best to bring everything we need from the houses outside onto the grounds near the campsite, so that it really seems as though we are camping as opposed to just being in a tent outside the main house. Part of the activity during the day is to gather sticks and logs for the camp fire that we will sit around at night. Our mothers also bring out tables and the food for dinner and breakfast; dinner is usually very simple, mainly hot dogs, hamburgers, corn on the cob, cooked on two coal pots; breakfast is scrambled eggs, bacon and Granny's famous banana bread. We put all of our food and drinks in a large cooler to avoid having to go inside to use the fridge. Going into the house spoils the camping feeling and we try our best to avoid it. The only thing we go inside for is to use the toilet. Other than that, we stay outside and use the outside shower next to the caretaker's shed.

Once, during one of our camping nights, a fat hairy tarantula fell out of a tree and landed on one of the tents that the Twins and Cakes were sleeping in with Uncle Dennis. They screamed so loudly they even woke up our grandparents, who barely heard anything. After that, my mother Bella forbade me to camp outside for the rest of the vacation and it took an entire year of begging to get her to agree to let me go outside to camp again with my father, Uncle Denny and my cousins.

At night, when we camp, we play cards around a portable table and sit on beach chairs; our only light comes from smelly kerosene lanterns, torch lights, the moon and stars. The card game is either All Fours or Fish, because the Twins like to shout "Go Fish!" in unison. Sometimes our fathers let us play way past our normal bedtime and they just sit around and have drinks around the camp fire. All of the beers, scotch and sodas are in their special adult cooler. The mothers are banned from coming to the campsite; this is meant to be father and daughter time, but it doesn't always work out that way. My mother Bella always finds some excuse to come outside and check on us. Sometimes Grandpa Alex joins us, and we like this because he always has stories to tell us about the trouble our mothers got into when they were young girls like us. Strangely enough, Aunt Juliette gave a lot more trouble as a teenager that the other two; she was the one who would try to run away to see a movie with friends and who had the first boyfriend. Grandpa Alex always made us promise not to let our mothers know that he had told us these stories and we'd swear to a camping code that we were never supposed to break. We'd fall asleep to the sound of the waves crashing on the rocks and our fathers' laughter drifting in and out of our tents.

All four of us often end up in one tent and the fathers are left to occupy the other. Blasts of sunlight make the tent hot in the mornings and the Twins' feet end up in our faces because they have managed to turn themselves around like a clock. We wake up groggy, hungry and hot, ready to get a warm breakfast of scrambled eggs, bacon, sausages and warm grilled bread with lots of butter and sweetened hot cocoa. Our mothers come out to the camp site early in the morning to prepare this for us, because our fathers are usually still asleep. We are always made to go inside to use the bathroom and brush out teeth before we can eat anything. Our mothers spread a blanket on the ground to keep the ants away, put the beach chairs around the shaky table where we played card games the night before and everything tastes a million times better because we are eating outside under the almond trees.

RAINY DAYS

On rainy days the men spend most of the time on the long wide porch, sitting in their Adirondack chairs discussing politics, business, or just making a lot of stupid jokes. My grandmother, who always wanted to play Scrabble or Monopoly, would set up the dining table with the board games. On most days we ended up playing Monopoly. We have played so many times we know who we are from the moment we sit in our designated Monopoly chairs; I am the shoe, Cakes is the horse, the Twins play together so they are the hat, and our granny loves the car. Aunt Miri always plays with us; she loves the little dog. My mother and Aunt Juliette sometimes join us for Scrabble but they are not big fans of Monopoly, mainly because the game usually ends with a quarrel. The Twins are the main culprits; they start off well, making joint decisions about whether to buy Boardwalk or Park Place if the hat manages to land there, but as the game progresses and Cakes, as usual, begins to acquire more and more of the properties the Twins want, they begin to argue with each other especially if their hat does not land on St James Place. They are also unlucky when it comes to the "Kitty in the Middle". Granny usually wins this because she always manages to land on "Go". Cakes and I compete fiercely and this does not help matters because sometimes we use the Twins to get back at each other. You would think that after all the quarrelling we would never play together again, but somehow Granny convinces us that all of this laughter, fighting, goading, negotiating and sulking is the best part of the game.

The game goes on for hours. While we play our fathers and Grandpa wander in from time to time to top up their drinks and offer to make gin and tonics for the cooks (Aunt Juliette and my mother Bella) and the players (Aunt Miri and Granny). Aunt Juliette could never handle more than one drink, but the other women hold their own, especially Aunt Miri who prefers gin and coconut water – sacrilege according to Granny. We are allowed soft drinks on rainy days, even Coca Cola is permitted, even though Granny believes that the Americans put something in that black drink that causes brain damage.

Rainy day lunches are usually a feast. Aunt Juliette makes desserts for the angels according to Grandpa. My mother Bella makes the simplest meals seem extra special and everything always looks beautiful. The rainy day menu includes warm sticky buns for Granny and vanilla pound cake for Grandpa. The smell of cinnamon and vanilla fills the house and to this day the memory lingers – of rain, Monopoly, cinnamon, noise and so much laughter.

DAUGHTERS

Good Friday and I am sitting in the darkness; it is five am. The Stations of the Cross, *Via Dolorosa, Via Lucis* – words I can still recall as I hear the voices of the procession chanting the prayers, their voices echoing through the valley as they approach the church on the hill. The sound is both beautiful and haunting. It makes me remember Aunt Juliette singing in the small seaside church choir for Mass on Sunday mornings. We'd drive to the church in our best-pressed clothes, walk in solemnly (no giggling allowed – or expect a hard pinch from any parent nearby) behind Grandpa Alex and Granny, proud patriarch and matriarch of the clan who lead us up to the third pew from the altar. The church was always full on Sunday mornings, mainly with the local villagers and a few others like us from town who had come to spend the August holidays at their seaside homes. The Monkey Boys and their parents didn't always attend mass, and this was another thing Grandpa Alex held against them. Not because he was particularly religious, but because they wouldn't hear his daughter sing. Aunt Juliette never sat with us, she was always seated on the side pews with the rest of the church choir made up primarily of older men and women from the village. She stuck out from the other choir members with her simple town clothes, which had less ruffles and lace than the other ladies, and with her younger looks and lighter complexion, but when they sang her voice blended perfectly with theirs. Sometimes Aunt Juliette sang alone for special occasions like a wedding or funeral. Her voice was delicate, yet piercing, like a violin. When she sang her shyness disappeared and someone else seemed to enter her, someone who was full of courage, no longer the quiet, shy aunt we all knew. Then, just as the music and singing stopped, it was as if a spell had worn off and the old Aunt Juliette returned. My Aunt Miri used to tease her sister about being Grandpa Alex's favourite daughter because she had such a beautiful voice. This made Grandpa Alex laugh; he enjoyed the competition amongst the sisters, but Aunt Juliette did not like it at all; it drew attention to her and she hated this most of all.

When we were growing up, my cousins and I always felt as though we had three mothers, Bella, Miri and Juliette. They all talked in the same way with only slight differences in intonation. Sometimes, like the Twins, they even confused our grandparents. But we knew the differences: Aunt Miri spoke with just a little more firmness, with long sentences and even longer words; my mother Bella was the most diplomatic of the three; she could hold her own with Aunt Miri but would often give in to keep the peace; Aunt Juliette said little but when she did speak, usually in few words and simple terms, she was often right.

Even as children we saw how all three daughters, including my mother Bella, bathed in Grandpa Alex's attention; he adored them all, but in different ways and for different things. He talked to Aunt Miri the most. She loved to argue and challenge Grandpa. They both read more books than the rest of us. With Aunt Miri we played the dictionary game for a prize, usually for four blocks of chocolate – Aunt Miri always had a stash of Cadbury; the other reward was cash. Sometimes, as the eldest, I had to look for and memorise two words. Cakes and the Twins usually got one. I always went first with the folded

paper Aunt Miri would hand us. I would run as fast as I could
to Grandpa's enormous, worn, heavy, blue Oxford dictionary
that was always on an old wooden book shelf in the living
room. I had five to ten minutes to find the words, memorise
them and run back with the answer to Aunt Miri. Each
memorised word earned a red dollar or the blocks of chocolate.
Cakes and I usually opted for the cash because we knew that the
Twins would take the chocolate and then we could beg them
for a block or two. Poor Twins, they seldom told us no. Some
afternoons, when we had nothing else to do, we would sit and
listen to Aunt Miri and Grandpa discuss books or politics, or
other things that were usually of no interest to us. But we liked
to hear them battle it out until there was a clear winner; and if
Grandpa gave in with a smile and a nod – which was rare – Aunt
Miri would beam for the rest of the day.

   All three daughters were pretty to us, but in different ways.
Aunt Miri took after Granny in looks; her skin was smooth, her
eyes were almond-shaped, her eyelashes long and thick –
which made them look fake, like a doll's. She was also tall and
lean like Granny, but the most outstanding feature was her
long, thick dark hair that always seemed to shine. My Aunt
Juliette's looks went well with her voice. Unlike Aunt Miri's
striking features, Aunt Juliette's face had the stillness of a
painting, like a beautiful portrait that you lingered on and grew
to love even more over time. My mother Bella, lived up to her
name, but it was both a blessing and a curse for her. Her eyes
were the most striking feature; sometimes they looked green
and at other times a light brown, and because her skin was
darker than her sisters it created an even more beautiful
contrast. If only her looks had given her enough courage to face
the world without anxiety and worry. She was always afraid of
disappointing everyone, but mostly herself. Grandpa had tried,
where my grandmother had failed, to make Bella believe that

everything would be fine, but it was a hard sell. Her time with Grandpa was spent talking about the day-to-day things in life that worried her; my grandmother was often impatient with my mother's worries. Granny prided herself on her resilience and it irritated and pained her to see my mother suffer. Grandpa tried to fill my mother's mind with other things. I remember overhearing my mother say to Grandpa that I was one more thing to worry about. She may not have said it in those words but that is how I remember it. They were sitting on Grandpa's favourite spot on the porch looking out to the sea. For a long time it made me feel like a burden; later in life, as a mother myself, I understood her fears. Neither of my grandparents knew where this worrying had come from. My grandmother said that some people were born worriers and others we born warriors; only two types in this world. Maybe. But I also learned that it was not always easy to pick out the worrier from warrior. If you looked at my grandparents you would have thought that Grandpa, who usually sounded bothered and irritated, was the warrior and my grandmother, whose face always glowed with warmth and graciousness, was the worrier, but the reverse was true.

Both Granny and Grandpa came together like a strange stew in Aunt Juliette. She had the most elegant hands and fingers. Sometimes, when she liked a piece of music she would wave them in the air, slowly – waltzing with her fingers, Grandpa used to say. Her two older sisters protected their little sister and always referred to her as their baby sister, long after anyone could think of her as a baby. Aunt Juliette hid her powers well; she didn't argue like Aunt Miri, or worry like my mother Bella; but she knew when she was needed most. She was the one who, when our grandparents died, helped, in her quiet way, to organise everything: the funeral home, the burial plot, the programme for the funeral and even the caterers for the house after the funeral. Aunt Miri and my mother Bella helped of course, but it was Aunt Juliette who carried us all through those deaths, Grandpa first and Granny a year later, almost to the day.

At the seaside, Aunt Juliette and Grandpa spent most of their time together listening to music. The main house had a record player and Grandpa's wide collection of records. Grandpa, unlike Granny, was not a big fan of classical music; he preferred other classics, the great greats, Grandpa called them: Nat King Cole, Louis Armstrong, Ella Fitzgerald, Frank Sinatra. The great greats also included calypsonians like the Mighty Lion, Lord Kitchener and the Mighty Sparrow. The main house always had music flowing through it and we would often hear Granny telling Grandpa to turn it down, that this was not a bar, and why couldn't he play something a little more soothing. Aunt Juliette and Grandpa listened to music on the porch, he in his Adirondack chair with the faded blue and white striped cushions, Aunt Juliette next to him.

★

As the light begins to enter the living room, the voices from the procession fade. I imagine them entering the church now, in a line. What station is this? Where is the cross? I can't remember; it's been so long and, unlike my cousins, I seldom go to church now.

My Stella's suitcases are at the bottom of the stairwell and she will soon come down, beautiful, dressed and ready to leave me. My role is to give her breakfast, make sure she has all of her documents for travel and get her to the airport on time. Her father will meet her on the other side, at Gatwick and help her to settle into her apartment in Putney. All of this has been carefully planned for months. Christopher's copyright conference dates coincide with her arrival to start her internship at a publishing house in London. I wanted to be the one there with her but my role as daughter has trumped that of mother. I have to stay behind to take care of my mother who is very ill. Stella has cousins in London and friends from university to help her. She won't be alone but I will.

SOLD

"Matura! Balandra! Rampanalgas! Cumana! Toco! Sans Souci! Grand Rivere! Matelot!" We shout out the list in a chorus, all four of us, Cakes, the Twins and yours truly, on our afternoon drives in Grandpa's old wagon. Cakes and I usually remember all of names of the seaside villages, but the Twins just mime the words. Sometimes Grandpa would make us start from the town of Valencia, but my grandmother would take our side, arguing that Valencia was not a seaside village so it didn't count. He made our mothers do the same thing when they were young and Aunt Miri always won the prize. Aunt Miri told us the prize was the privilege of getting to sit in the front seat with Grandpa on longer, special drives to the Toco Lighthouse or to explore the Matelot river.

The drive from the North West where we lived to the seaside compound in Balandra took about two hours, but it felt like four. The cars, Grandpa and Granny's, my father's, Uncle Denny's, and Aunt Miri's (she insisted on driving herself up to the beach so she could move around "how and when she wanted") were all packed and stuffed with boxes of food to feed ten armies: sheets, pillows, pillow cases, clothes, bikes, medical supplies for two hospitals and anything else that my mother, Aunt Juliette and Granny could stuff into the trunks. My father would always remind my mother that the house already had all the linen we would ever need in the store rooms, but it didn't seem to matter. He also reminded my mother that we were not moving up there for the rest of our lives but for a few weeks. None of this mattered. She still stuffed my father's station wagon, barely allowing him to see through the back of the vehicle in the rear-view mirror.

This over-packing has made me a light packer, but my daughter Stella has inherited her grandmother Bella's desire to carry everything. She has already sent across books, clothes and ordered more furniture online than she needs. Her father, more than I, indulges her and now that she is leaving us, gives her even more leeway than usual. I think it is his way of coming to terms with the fact that his daughter is leaving. He refuses, though, to discuss the emptiness to come.

Last year, the family decided to organise a reunion at the compound. We had all decided that it was time to put the property on the market. As beautiful as it was, we seldom used it anymore and had been renting the main house as a way to pay for maintenance of the whole property. No one said it, but we had all found it difficult to go to the property since our grandparents died. They had both lived long enough to enjoy the houses until their deaths – Grandpa at ninety-four and Granny at ninety-two. The compound had never been the same without them and the family had spread itself around the globe. Aunt Juliette and Uncle Denny had left to live in London where they would be closer to their children and grandchildren; Cakes had two boys, the Twins a girl each. Aunt Miri had also left for Texas to live with Burt-the-American.

For a few years after their deaths, the family had tried to keep up the August holiday tradition. One or another family member would visit and we would go up to the houses, but no matter how many people were there, guests and family, it always felt empty. We missed Grandpa Alex's booming voice giving instructions to everyone and Granny's wide smile.

Their absence haunted us. The family had moved through both funerals in a trance. Grandpa Alex and Granny had been the centre of our lives, even more than our own parents, and we felt lost for a long time, rudderless, adrift.

So the entire clan made an effort for this last reunion on the compound; there was a buyer and soon the compound would no longer belong to us. There were many trips back and forth to the airport, to meet with cousins, sisters, uncles, children, grandchildren. We had grown and Grandpa and Granny would have loved to have seen the many generations. I was overjoyed to see Stella with her cousins, it reminded me of how special it was as an only child to have had Cakes and the Twins; they had been sisters more than cousins.

For the reunion lunch we tracked down two of the three Monkey Boys, their wives and their own children. One of the Monkey Boys, Simon, had actually gone to the same high school and had been in the same year as my future husband. An island is a small place and a seaside village on an island is even smaller. My mother Bella had found some of the choir members who sang with Aunt Juliette and this pleased Aunt Juliette beyond measure.

We made it an occasion Granny and Grandpa would have been proud of. The menu included all of dishes that my granny liked to prepare. There were certain recipes that she had taken to the grave, so we had to rely on our taste memory and our dear old housekeeper, Bernie, to help us. The main dish was Granny's famous red fish with her special stuffing of ginger, carrots, onions, bread crumbs and something else – a secret ingredient that only Bernie knew about. To go with the fish we had perfect, fluffy white rice with melted butter, her special pigeon peas with pumpkin, and a thick slice of ripe avocado with a light vinaigrette. It was simple, delicious, and a king's feast for Grandpa. For dessert it was always homemade coconut ice cream that we used to churn as children in a wooden bucket, adding salt to the ice and waiting for Granny to order us to stop so we could check to see if it was ready. This stopping to taste was worth the hard work, a little of the salt from the ice always seemed to get into the sweetened milk mixture and this made it all the more delicious.

For the reunion lunch we cheated and bought the coconut ice cream; the guests brought other desserts to add to the feast. We drank rum punch. Burt-the-American had too many and retired early, even though he had been warned about the dangers of local rum. There were many gin and tonics, some with bitters, some with thin slices of lime, and everyone toasted Granny and Grandpa with champagne. After lunch, when most of us were a little tipsy, we danced to all the music Grandpa and Aunt Juliette loved. In the evening, we moved the party to the porch of the main house. Grandpa loved to see the rocks disappearing as the darkness spread over his part of the ocean. One by one we faded, spread ourselves across the three houses, drifted off to a sweet sleep having taken as much as we could from the day.

The morning before we left the compound, we drove in a convoy towards the Toco lighthouse. The first stop was the Rough Beach where the currents had always been too danger-ous for swimming. As children we had spent many afternoons running along the wet grainy sand of the Rough Beach. We pretended not to hear the cries of my mother Bella and Granny begging us not to go too close to the water, as though the waves had giant hands that could pull us in and carry us out towards the horizon. Grandpa loved that beach and Aunt Miri wanted to show Burt where she had taken so many walks with her father as they discussed how they would solve all the world's problems. Of the three sisters, Aunt Miri talked about Granny and Grandpa the most. Aunt Juliette didn't say much about

them, and my mother just seemed to worry about her sisters'
sadness, probably to avoid her own.

The Toco lighthouse turned out to be the biggest disappointment of the weekend; the place looked run down. The
benches and chairs were broken, the toilets were filthy, there
were plastic bottles and old boxes of chicken and chips scattered across the grounds. It was an embarrassment for us to
imagine what Burt must have thought. The place was ne-
glected and abandoned. Still, when we walked onto the rocks,
turning our backs on the unkempt surroundings, some of the
disappointment was replaced by the strong winds and stagger-
ing view of the sea.

We left the compound at the usual time we always left on a
Sunday afternoon – around three pm. After it was sold I could
never go back.

STICK NO BILLS

The day before my daughter left I drove past the old ice factory. That place and my mother always went together. As a child, I loved the factory wall even more than the inside of the factory itself. The wall is dirtier these days, but it's still thick, rough and a blueish-grey that makes it seem as cold as the ice inside. My mother and I would go through the tall, black factory gates and drive to a raised platform where giant ice-factory men in dark overalls, big gloves and enormous ice picks (an image at once frightening and exciting to my young-girl eyes) would pull and drag huge blocks of ice across the ground and then put them into the back of my mother's station wagon. She was the one who bought the ice for the parties at our house – and my parents were always entertaining.

Facing the the roadway, the ice factory wall had a small phrase repeatedly stencilled in black: **STICK NO BILLS**. I am not sure why I loved that sign so much but I did. I didn't even know then what it meant – what were bills? The cold-looking wall and the stencilled signs are still there, along with the memory of my mother and me inside the factory wall buying ice.

Another favourite sign for me as a child was the one around the Savannah, near the Queen's Park Hotel: **Four Taxis Facing North** – although it could have been five.

Recently I've been passing another sign on a dilapidated house. It must have been charming once but it has deteriorated over the years; the wooden latticework above the door and around the windows is chipped and cracking; the white paint is greying; and the wooden columns holding up the steps leading to the entrance look like the thinning legs of an old lady. The entire house leans to one side, even as the sign at its pinnacle says *Hope*. The word affects me differently, depending on the way I see my life that day. Like that house, I am trying hard not to let my own paint crack too much on a surface that no longer has the smooth, clear glow of youth. Knowing that my daughter was going soon made everything more difficult. Knowing that my mother was leaving us as well made these days seem to go by even faster, though I was trying to slow them down.

Whenever I had difficulties at school my mother would always find the right words to say to me. She hated to see me worried or anxious, maybe because she was afraid she had passed on all of her anxieties to me like a bad gene. She monitored our lives so carefully, afraid of them becoming disorganised. She planned all of our comings and goings, the big dates, the parties, the birthdays, marking all the important events, but sometimes missing the important details of the moment. I have tried to mother my daughter differently, but have come to understand my mother's desire to control everything she could. Now, I understand that underlying fear and that primal instinct to protect your child from inevitable pain.

3: LOST AND FOUND

For my parents, Margaret and Derek

"The robb'd that smiles steals something from the thief"
— *Othello*

GUESTS

She was dressed, ready to greet her guests. Hair combed, bathed, powdered and creamed, even a little bit of perfume. She sat on the chair propped higher with two cushions and greeted them warmly as they entered. Earlier in the day she had eaten her porridge, her soup, her fruit; she had eaten well that day and everyone was happy. She wanted more sweet things but they didn't give them to her; she wanted to drink a fizzy drink but they said no. She waited. Two by two they came, sat and chatted, or stared at the television. They were served cold drinks and a few laughs. They talked about everything else for as long as they could before they finally asked what the doctors had said.

She smiled and gave them the answer to the question that she knew by heart now, the same one she had given to all the visitors who had come before, and as they grew a little sadder she tried to console them: "One day at a time," she said, "one day at a time."

82

Curtains, open, light, birds, morning, lawn, bougainvillea,
veranda, dogs, coconuts, oranges, palms, fronds, ceiling, fan,
chair, bed, bedding, box, glasses, pills, water, straws, scarfs,
comb, smooth, skin, cream, face, brush, thrush, pillows, head,
up, night, sleep, tight, lollies, laughter, hands, veins, hold,
grand, daughters, sons, ice, pack, sock, sit, slippers, bathe,
chair, hair, bones, eyes, dim, talk, hugs, news, nurse, book, TV,
record, tubes, breath, breathe, pupils, stare, white, sheet, roll,
body, flower, sour, sower, ash, Wednesday, words, dusk, dawn,
good, gone.

ONE DAY AT A TIME

You cannot sleep beyond six am, no matter what, so you get up,
you do everything the same way: fumble for your slippers
without your glasses, find your glasses, throw down the alarm
clock, he groans, you pick up the alarm clock, feel your way to
the bathroom, switch on the light, wash face, pee, wash hands,
brush teeth, wash face again, fix ridiculous hair, go downstairs.
Take your vitamins, put on the kettle for coffee – too addicted
to coffee – toast in toaster, bread, butter, guava jam, more
coffee, birds chirping, dogs barking. The valley is waking up,
the valley is stretching.

And then what you think you have forgotten is what you
remember when you are finally awake, because you know now
you could probably spend a lifetime walking in your sleep, eyes
focused on nothing, moving through spaces, places, hours,
doing what has to be done, just the necessary to survive. The
background noise is what you forget, or simply neglect, so early
in the morning when days follow days with no real beginning
or end.

WAITING

That haunting feeling was always there, it never left her no matter what she did, and once the busyness of the moment was over she felt it again. An incomplete feeling of something that needed to be done, or something that she had forgotten to do, forever nagging and gnawing at her. Haunted best described it; this feeling so much a part of who she was. She had lived with it for so long she expected it to be there still lingering, making her forever ill-at-ease with herself. She felt she had earned a promised peace, had done everything she thought she was supposed to do on that never ending list, but the disquiet always returned. Still, there had been moments of lightness: a sixteenth birthday party, the birth of a child, a wedding day. Now she knew what it was. From the window she could see the gate and it occurred to her that she was waiting, a fool's hope, for them to walk through it.

THAT WHITE HORSE

The white horse appeared in the Savannah hollows like a beautiful ghost, in the morning, around seven am. A woman held the horse while it was grazing. On one side there was the early morning traffic, rushing past the turn-off to Lady Chancellor Hill and on the other side the beautiful horse. I looked down at a carpet of pink flowers on the ground; we were in the dry season; these pink Pouis would soon be followed by the yellow, the Savannah showing off its most beautiful self.

When I looked up again the horse and the lady were gone, and I wondered whether they had ever been there. When I told you this story you said that I had imagined it; you always made fun of my imaginings. So, the next day I went to the Savannah at the same time and to same place looking for the white horse and the lady. They disappeared for a few days and I began to doubt myself. Perhaps you were right; once again I had seen something I wanted to see. But just as I was about to give up hope, just before I completed my walk, there they were, the white horse and the lady, not in the Savannah hollows but at another spot, further inside. I never told you about seeing them again because I didn't want her to stop sending me these signs, telling me that she was fine and in some place just as beautiful.

BRIDGES
(for Anna)

When I was a girl, young enough to feel small in my mother's car, I was afraid of crossing bridges. Afraid that we would fall, my sister Anna and I, into the river down below and never make it to the other side. I imagined the bridge shaking, creaking, breaking, crumbling and that would be all. It was a ticklish fear, a mixture of excitement and dread, butterflies and something else I cannot really describe. So I loved and hated it at the same time. But somewhere inside I knew that we could trust her to get us over safely, bridge after bridge, every time. That fear still lingers, pops up from time to time, I know it's not real, maybe it's just nostalgia for a memory, or a mother, both beyond my reach now, both on the other side.

SATURDAY MORNINGS ON THE HILL
(for Joanne, Tracy, Corinna, Jen and Giselle)

Most Saturday mornings I run up that hill, sometimes alone, sometimes with friends who have become bright lights in my life. When I am alone, the hill is always harder, but there is more space for thoughts. Sometimes too many come at once and I lose my stride, my rhythm. Thoughts can do that, affect breathing; running, like life, is all about the breath.

On Saturday mornings the hill is crowded with all types: runners, walkers, riders, children in prams, groups, loners, couples – all trying to get to the top. There are luxurious homes tucked into the hillside and trees shade us for much of the climb. "Morning" we say, or simply nod to acknowledge a fellow climber. With each bend, especially on a sunny morning, the Savannah down below glistens and even the charmless buildings of that charmless capital with its dirty harbour shine.

The other morning, running alone, I saw someone I knew; she smiled in her usual wide, lovely, quiet way. She wore a wide-rimmed black hat to protect her pale skin from the sun. In her black tee-shirt and long, lose, black pants she stood out as she walked past a group in fluorescent gym wear. The hill has no dress code, we all belong and are free to wear whatever we like; no one really cares. My friend was heading up as I was going down, having already run to the top, performed my ritual at the top of the hill of touching the spot on our magic tree, always taking a moment to look at the pines along the ridge on the next hill. These, like soldiers, stand in a line, protecting the valleys below.

At the top of the hill, when I am with my friends, after we touch the trunk, we always congratulate each other, as though it were our first time to get to the top, even though it's been many years since we started to spend Saturday mornings together. They don't know that these days when I get to the top I always think of you.

My friend in the wide black hat had recently lost her husband. I used to see them out together; they were always together. Black is our colour of mourning; the words morning and mourning; their sound is so unfairly similar. On the way down I pass others I know. This one has just lost a brother, this one a mother. My friend is not alone; we all share in some loss and these glorious Saturday mornings on the hill.

JACMEL

How many islands have places with the same names? How many Jacmels? How many St Annes? Soufrières? Diamants? We were laughing in the car making jokes about the Europeans' lack of imagination and by Europeans we really meant the colonisers and by colonisers we really meant the French and Spanish and by the French and Spanish we really meant the Catholics.

It was midmorning and we were driving to the St Lucian Jacmel, not the Haitian one. We drove up that steep hill leaving Castries, over the winding roads, over more hills, passing the small towns you adored, slowly making our way to our destination. We were going to that beautiful church at the end of that short road in the middle of the valley we all loved. It felt as though we were in a painting surrounded by so many shades of green with patches of silver as the sun lit up parts of the banana plantation. You worshipped that landscape because it was poetry, worthy of much better words than these, but I was not the poet and you had already captured it for all of us so perfectly.

At the church they led us to the front and we sat in the pew close to the altar. Your old friend's glorious mural faced us, with a St Lucian Madonna and child, workers in the fields, dancers, a holy family. We were here to celebrate his birthday and the *Jounen Kwèyòl*, or *Journée Créole*. In the packed church, almost everyone wore something in madras to acknowledge the special day. The preacher preached in Creole and English, switching effortlessly from one tongue to the other. As he spoke of sinners, I thought of how easy it was in French to confuse a *pêcheur* with a *pécheur,* to *pêcher* or *pécher*; one little accent could make a fisherman a sinner. And was that so far away from a *prêcheur*?

At the end of the mass there was a traditional dance. Two lines were formed on either side of the pews; on one side the young men from Jacmel, flawless in their crisp white shirts, pressed black trousers and madras sash; on the other, a line of pretty young girls in white cotton blouses, their *chimiz decolté*, long white skirts, their *jips* or *jupes* trimmed with the *bodwi angléz, broderie anglaise*; their shorter madras skirts worn over longer white skirts, and their madras head-ties matching their skirts. They were perfection. Each movement of the dance simple, graceful, innocent. The young men bowed and dipped as the girls swayed their skirts; it recalled a past that most of us had forgotten and I thought I saw the preacher and the rest of us sinners trying to not cry.

That night, as if the day had not been perfect enough, there was a full moon, but before that we had wine around dusk, looking out across the bay to Pigeon Island. We spoke about the church, community, communion and how in the old days some people would fast before receiving the host. So I raised my glass to make a toast, a toast to my hosts. We chinked our glasses and the silliness brushed away my fear for a moment, that new fear I carried with me everywhere, but mostly here with you. It was the fear of not knowing how much longer we had together. One had left me already, when would the other?

CASE EN BAS
(for David)

"Love is so short, forgetting so long" Pablo Neruda

You led, I followed and we went back and forth like this along the main road. It was mid-morning, blazing light, sticky heat and the main street was already busy; taxis swerving in and out, groups huddled at the bus stop, cars lining up at the gas station. It was just too hot for a run; we should have left earlier. Running along the beach was nice; we had the sea almond trees, then through Gros Islet, a little more shade, but after that the crowded road. Two crazy people running at this hour; only tourists did stupid things like that, and we were not tourists, though not exactly local, not American, not European, but Caribbean like them. This place was not my home and yet it was, or could have been; I had roots here, family buried here, a part of me could easily lay claim to somewhere here.

But you ran ahead as though you saw a clear a path on this jungle of a street. Not to worry, you said, we'll turn off soon and get away from these kamikaze drivers. They seemed irritated by two lunatics willingly running through a furnace while everyone else was trying to shelter from a sky on fire. I couldn't blame them, I would have been irritated as well. *Get a job, get a life, what gives you the right to be on vacation while we have to suffer?* It wasn't even summer or winter, not even tourist time of year.

Before too long we turned off the main road onto one of the side streets. The morning before you got lost trying to find a new place for us to explore and now you wanted to find out where you had gone wrong by retracing your steps. That was the difference between us; you liked to go back and correct the errors so that you wouldn't make the same mistake again. I preferred to ignore, to forget.

The side road was less crowded. We passed a young man going to work and a young boy in school uniform: khaki shorts, blue shirt, black insignia on the pocket; a universal Caribbean uniform found on any island. The boy, eight or nine, was he heading out to get a taxi to school, or maybe to walk there? No parent in sight, so young to be on his own. There were a few houses, some trees but it was hilly, undulating. I liked to run hills but the heat made it harder. We hugged the side of the road where the broad branches offered some relief; the shade was like a sip of cool water.

"That was where I turned off yesterday; I thought it would take me down to the beach," you said, pointing to a road that led to a dam. We had turned off of that horrible main road, but I still wasn't happy with the run; it was not like the one we had done together two days before. That was planned. We left earlier in the morning and I felt ready for that run, but this morning, because of the night before, because of the night ahead, my thoughts were controlling my stride and my legs felt like logs.

St Lucian mud is not regular mud, it is a deep blackish-brown, and it sticks and clings to your shoes like some alien creature, pulling you back down towards the earth. Running on this mud is always difficult, frustrating and in the rainy season it is even worse.

"Shit," the first thing I'd said since we left the main road, "This damn frigging mud." You were now alongside of me because we had turned off the road with the damn-frigging mud and were definitely on a trail, still muddy, with holes, stones, some garbage in between the trees, and an abandoned car.

"After this it gets better." You were still trying to reassure me because you knew that I was not enjoying it, and even though you hated the mud as well, you still managed to keep going. This faith you have in everything, in life, in me, I have never understood it.

"It will turn off and get back to the path we were on yesterday," you said. "Not yesterday. Remember, I didn't come with you yesterday; it was the day before. Yesterday, you got lost." I said this to remind you that you were not perfect; anyone could get lost, even you, known for your amazing sense of direction – of which I had none. You could visit a place once and remember the route; I could go there a million times and still never find it again. That was why you wanted to come back, to get it right and live up to your reputation. It had nothing to do with me, it had everything to do with you. But you didn't respond to my attack, you didn't fall for the trap, you just kept running and pulled ahead just slightly, no longer alongside me.

The path got a little better; we passed a rusting yellow tractor and two wooden shacks, with rotting galvanized roofs. There was a Rasta in the distance who may have waved at us but I wasn't sure. The mud was still pulling at my feet. When we ran by puddles of water I stopped for a moment and tried to wash some of it off. You waited for me, "We still have a lot of mud to go through." I raised my shoulders, a shrug meaning so what, I'm fed up already.

When we turned again I finally recognized the stony road, the one we *had* taken before to get us to the beach, the one that we had used on so many other occasions to drive down in my uncle's jeep. "You know where you are now?" he said. I thought: I never know where I am, not now, not ever. "Always lost," was what I said, but you knew that my heavy mood was lifting, just in time for the soft sea breeze that filled the air with that potent seaside smell.

You were back alongside of me and even let me go ahead and lead. The morning before, after your run, you brought back freshly baked, warm Creole bread to have with butter and sweetened black St. Lucian coffee. I loved the nutmeg jelly as well and we sat and ate a late breakfast on the small veranda with a view of the sea and rocks. You were hoping that this would cheer me up after the news from the doctors. There were so many things wrong with my uncle's body, my uncle who was like a father to me. They'd sent him home from the hospital but we didn't know if that meant that they could do no more or that he was actually getting a little better. He was stable now, they had said, so he can go home. You adored my uncle almost as much as I did; you knew that he was the one who, after my mother remarried, had given me the best life he could possibly afford to give. This was more than a beautiful home and things; my mother had given me all of that already. What my uncle gave was something more; he restored some of the faith I had lost.

The weather was changing again, brighter, windier and the smell of the sea was even stronger. It was all downhill from here, down to *Case en bas*, at least that is what I thought. But you turned off to the side.

"Come this way, this will get us to the place with the tents and the flags, to the edge of that point." You showed me the direction, then took off your cap and wiped your shaven head, ran your fingers over your thick black eyebrows. You were sweating, dripping, so you wiped your face again, raising your shirt just above your stomach, enough for me to see your beautiful torso. It was always fairer than the rest of your body which was a dark golden brown, and I realised how much I was still attracted to you even after all of this time, after these years battling life together. You never cared about how you looked; you just wanted to stay strong and healthy enough to do all that you wanted to do. Life was short and you didn't believe in another, so time here was all we had, and no one knew how much of it. Work was just a means to another end, a way to travel, run, ride and explore; to see as many landscapes as you could, old world and new, castles and caves. And you wanted me to come with you. You were as fearless as I was afraid, always with this trust, this ridiculous trust.

The path was beginning to widen and the trees turned into brush, opening up to a clear sky. The sea was right there; I could hear it crashing against the rocks. We got to a barricade across the path with a rusted chain and lock, a fading sign above with the warning: "Private Property. Trespassers Will Be Pros-ecuted." But without hesitation you held up the chain link and helped me to pass underneath the barricade.

"I wonder who owns this place?" I asked. You didn't hear or just didn't care. We ran a little faster even though the ground was rockier, drier; we were running to that opening, to the sound of the ocean, the Atlantic on this side of the island. My uncle's house was on the other side, the Caribbean side. It was calmer and the colour was a lighter green; the Atlantic, a deeper hue of blue and the water rougher, the waves like tall walls.

There was another large wooden log a little higher up. You stepped over it and held out your hands to help me across. I gave you my water bottle and asked again, "I wonder who owns this land?" This time, as though hearing me for the first time, you responded. The morning before you had met an old man who said he owned a few acres closer to the ocean, that he had recognised you from a few years ago when you were riding along the ridge. Even though I'd asked, I didn't pay close

attention to your story about the old man because the space
before us was distractingly beautiful – a wide, windy plain that
led straight to the edge of the rocky cliff and from there to the
Atlantic. Tall cacti were scattered around us and the ground
was rocky, dry, a brownish green colour.

"Be careful where you step." You pointed to the heaps of
cow or horse dung because there were many wild horses in this
area of the island, especially beyond the cliffs of *Case en bas*. We
had seen wild horses on the run we took together a few days
before.

We walked all the way to the edge of the cliff. On the left and
right we could see the long stretches of beach below. On one
side there were white huts, their bright flags flittering in the
wind. At the side of the huts, trees with bent trunks looked as
though they were bowing to the god of the wind. You said that
the huts were originally used by soldiers in training, but now
they were used for scouts, or campers, or surfers – anyone, if
they got   permission. I wondered how you had got this
information; maybe the old man.

Both of us were silent for a while, just trying to take in this
wonder before us. "This would be a great place for a house, just
us, the sea and no other humans." You smiled, agreeing with
me. We even decided on a perfect spot for our imaginary home
and it reminded me of when we were first married. We would
go on adventures like this to other islands, finding places that
would make beautiful homes, always near the sea, always far
away from everyone.

From this height the sea took on different shades of blue,
green, then emerald, and we could see patterns and shadows on
water's surface.

"Let's go down to the beach," you said, so we ran down
carefully, avoiding the sharp rocks. At the bottom, the first part
of the beach was covered with flat black stones along the

shoreline, and the sea made a rumbling sound as it moved back and forth over these stones. The ones closer to the water glistened like onyx, those closer to the shore were drier, more grey than black. We had to walk over the stones, trying our best not to get our running shoes wet, but it was pointless, we couldn't avoid the water. Further down the beach there were mounds of old, brown, greying sea weed; the scent was salty, musty and so pungent. The intertwined fine, curly strands of grey seaweed reminded me of my uncle's hair and I thought of him again at home in bed with bottles of water, cups and pills where his books should have been.

"We'll run up a little more," you said, "to get another view of the bay." I followed you off the beach and up through the sea grapes. As we got to a hilly spot you held my hand to pull me up. I felt your rough palms from working in so many gardens, long fingers, elegant yet strong. I had run out of water and you let me pull from your Camelback straw.

It had been at least two hours since we had left my uncle's home and it was time to get back. We always had lunch with him and my aunt, even though some days he was too weak to come to the table.

We didn't go back the same way. This time we took a more familiar route, one that I knew, so I lead. When you saw the empty hut, the *case,* you were reminded again of the old man, the one that you had seen the day before and so many years ago. Then, as if on cue, an old man appeared in the distance with a long walking stick in one hand, a light brown sack on one shoulder with two sticks sticking out at the top. He wore a greying vest, worn khaki shorts and a tattered Boston Red Sox baseball cap.

"That's him, the same one." You looked so happy to see him.

As he approached, we slowed down to greet him. Good mornings were exchanged and you told him that I was your wife. The old man said he was late getting to his land that morning because he had been taking care of *his* wife who was very sick and needed medicine. He looked worried and sad when he said this. You told him about our run to the other side where the huts were and the old man, revealing his toothless smile, said he was glad that we had had a good morning.

"Yes, it was good," you said, and I agreed nodding my head.

He was a handsome old man with watery, sea-green eyes that shone against his dark skin. Before we left, you told him that we were flying back to our home tomorrow.

"And me," the old man said, "I never been nowhere, only here, just happy here."

"Here is good place to be," you said.

The old man smiled again, then turned and continued walking up the hill. We ran down in the opposite direction, in stride, alongside each other.

LOST AND FOUND
(for Jeremy)

In order to help him I had to enter his dream. He was sitting, looking out at the bay from his chair. His eyes, the colour of the sea, fixed on some spot that only he could see. For a moment we were all there with him, children and grandchildren, standing behind him for a grand family portrait. But he didn't seem to notice us, he was looking for her. The battle, he had said, was not with the loss but with the forgetting. That is the fear we carry with us.

Another scene, we are all at the round table in the valley, laughing and arguing ideas to the death. This time she is there and so is he, younger versions of themselves. The bougainvillea purple, orange, fuchsia are overgrown, the table has a long crack down the centre, like a broken spine; it balances on three legs, the fourth fractured, like an injured dog. We act as though we will be sitting at that round table in our glistening valley forever, so we don't see it coming, too careless with our happiness, and soon the plants claim it all: house, chairs, beds and the sound of our voices.
    "What fades first?"
    "What do you lose first?"
    "Forgetting is the fear we carry with us."

Tap, tap, tapping as we have breakfast; playing your music on an imaginary keyboard. She is making scrambled eggs; we sit quietly and wait; you start a sentence and then you leave us. She completes it for you, fills in the space you left while you sit, tap, tap, tap. She measures sugar for your coffee, you measure lines. We wait and eventually you come back. We knew you would follow her, only a matter of time. The loss spread through you like a cancer; your words worked magic but only for a time, even your Paramin gods couldn't bring her back. What fades first is what we fear most, the little things we want to hold onto: battles at the breakfast table, pecks on the cheeks, the hellos and goodbyes. Healing and losing, finding peace in forgetting.

Misty, cool, dew-damp grass, sun coming up over the hill, my perfect morning. No longer running away, now I go towards it. Here and not here. I have stopped looking. Call off the search, sit at the table in that other valley with other voices, fresh and green like my morning.

Found.

ACKNOWLEDGMENTS

"Gros Islet" was published by *Babel* in Italian and published in *The Haunted Tropics Anthology* published by UWI Press; "Killing Time" was published in the on-line journal, *Caribbean Intransit*; "Cher Ami" was published in *The Missing Slate* on-line issue; "Ashes" was published in *New Daughters of Africa Anthology*; "Bridges" was published in *Bridges of Trinidad and Tobago*; "Jacmel" was published in *Caribbean Writer*.

Thanks to Amy Hackkshaw for the photo used on the cover.

ABOUT THE AUTHOR

Elizabeth Walcott-Hackshaw was born in Trinidad and is Professor of French Literature and Creative Writing at the University of the West Indies. She has coedited several works including *Border Crossings: A Trilingual Anthology of Caribbean Women Writers*, *Caribbean Research: Literature, Discourse and Culture*, *Echoes of the Haitian Revolution 1804-2004* and *Reinterpreting the Haitian Revolution and its Cultural Aftershocks (1804-2004)*. Apart from her scholarly essays and articles she has also published creative works; *Four Taxis Facing North*, her first collection of short stories, was published in 2007 and translated into Italian in 2010. *Four Taxis* was considered one of the best works of 2007 by the Caribbean Review of Books. Her first novel, *Mrs. B* was published by Peepal Tree Press in 2014. *Mrs B*, was short listed for the "Best Book Fiction" in The Guyana Prize for Literature Award for 2014. Her short stories have been widely translated and anthologized. Walcott-Hackshaw presently lives in the Santa Cruz Valley with her family. She is working on a book of essays on trauma in Caribbean fiction.

ALSO BY ELIZABETH WALCOTT-HACKSHAW

Four Taxis Facing North
ISBN: 9781845233471; pp. 171; pub. 2007, 2017; £9.99

In Trinidad, oil wealth supported the growth of probably the most prosperous and conspicuously consuming middle-class in the Caribbean. But there was a price to pay for the deepened social inequalities that resulted: a deep paranoia rooted in the fear of crime and social upheaval.

The recent plunge in world oil prices has left these people in a double bind. Travel and education overseas have given them tastes that weaken their attachment to Trinidad, yet they know that their privileges of race and class would disappear in North America. As one narrator acknowledges, in the US she's the only black girl in most of her classes, "though at home no one would call me black."

Four Taxis Facing North presents us with an intimate, human face to what it is like to be one of those middle class Trinidadians. These stories focus on characters from both sides of the social divide – and their infrequent and often uncomfortable interactions. Even as they are beset by fears about the future, the Walcott-Hackshaw's women are also busy with their responsibilities, their relationships with husbands, partners, children, friends and foes. They deal with absent, unfaithful or abusive husbands and display differing degrees of self and social awareness.

Hackshaw offers few comforting illusions. She explores characters who are not always sympathetic – and the title story imagines a Trinidad after a great social upheaval in which survival means life of the bleakest kind. But the twelve stories in this collection offer great clarity, a moral vision and a deeply satisfying exactness of language in the creation of characters across the divisions of Trinidadian society.

With an introduction by Lawrence Scott.

Mrs B.
ISBN: 9781845232313; pp.194; pub., 2014; £9.99

Ruthie's academic success has been Mrs. B's pride and joy, but as the novel begins, she and her husband Charles are on their way to the airport to collect their daughter who has had a nervous breakdown after an affair with a married professor.

Loosely inspired by Flaubert's *Madame Bovary*, *Mrs. B* focuses on the life of an upper middle-class family in contemporary Trinidad, who have, in response to the island's crime and violence, retreated to a gated community. Mrs. B (she hates the name of Butcher) is fast approaching fifty and her daughter Ruthie's return from university and the state of her marriage provoke her to some unaccustomed self-reflection. Like Flaubert's heroine Mrs. B's desires are often tied to the expectations of her social circle.

Elizabeth Walcott-Hackshaw writes with wit, with brutal honesty and with warmth for her characters, but the novel questions how far the Butcher clan's love of Trinidad as place – their hedonistic pleasure in their holiday houses "down the islands" – can carry them towards a deeper engagement with their fellow but less privileged islanders.

"...richly entertaining. Walcott-Hackshaw offers a vigorous, at times sizzling, prose that is grounded in local rhythms and allusions to the culture that is at once both the object of her love and also her main target."

Arnold Rampersad, *Trinidad Guardian*